Also by Sid Hite

Cecil in Space

Cecil in SPACE

Sid Hite

Henry Holt and Company   New York

7 8 3 1 9

Henry Holt and Company, Inc.
Publishers since 1866
115 West 18th Street
New York, New York 10011

Henry Holt is a registered
trademark of Henry Holt and Company, Inc.

Published in Canada by Fitzhenry & Whiteside Ltd.,
195 Allstate Parkway, Markham, Ontario L3R 4T8.

Library of Congress Cataloging-in-Publication Data
Hite, Sid.
Cecil in space / by Sid Hite.
p.   cm.
Summary: Seventeen-year-old Cecil tries to help his best friend, Isaac, who is under
suspicion of having vandalized the welcome sign at the edge of their small Virginia
town, and pursues his interest in Isaac's sister, Isabel.
[1. Vandalism—Fiction. 2. Friendship—Fiction. 3. Virginia—Fiction.] I. Title.
PZ7.H62964Ce   1999   [Fic]—dc21   98-36948

ISBN 0-8050-5055-8
First Edition—1999
Designed by Lilian Rosenstreich
Printed in the United States of Amer[...]
on acid-free paper. ∞
10 9 8 7 6 5 4 3 2

This is a work of fiction. The town of Bricksburg and the characters portrayed in this book are inventions of the author's imagination. Nevertheless, in an effort to protect the guilty, each name has been changed twice. Although all quotes from Sigmund Freud and references made to the work of Albert Einstein are valid, the same cannot be said for Krol Zandinsky. He never wrote a book called The Untold Universe. *It does not exist. Neither does Krol.*

Thanks to Michael Coffey for telling me a story about Peanut, a dog that cavorted with a fox and lived with a family of four boys in upstate New York.

Cecil in Space

Hysteric Bricksburg

Hello. My name is Cecil Scott Rowe. I'm three months past my seventeenth birthday, and I live in the small town of Bricksburg, Virginia. The place is a podunk, a boring little village set down in the middle of nowhere. The stores in town close at five. The gas station shuts at six. The streets are rolled up at seven and put in storage for the night.

There are few jobs in Bricksburg, and most people who have any ambition at all move away after high school. Many of them never return. Thus there's a dearth of young families with children in Bricksburg and the population is top-heavy with old folks. A large percentage of the old folks are crazy or so eccentric it's hard to tell the difference. Going crazy is the risk one runs when living in such a backwater. I'm not sure how I've managed to survive as long as I have.

The word *crazy* is a liberal term—it means different things to different people, depending on the context. According to *Webster's New Collegiate Dictionary*, it means: unsound, crooked, erratic, askew, out of the ordinary. Hmm. Just about everyone I know is out of the ordinary.

Although nothing important has ever happened here and probably never will, the good citizens of our town recently voted to erect a sign that says: Welcome to Historic Bricksburg. The premise for this communal delusion dates to the Civil War, when a Union scouting party accidentally stumbled upon a handful of Confederate troops camped three miles west of Bricksburg. There was an inconsequential exchange of gunfire that ended with the Northern troops retreating. No one was captured. No one was killed. Nevertheless, in utter disregard for the truth (the incident didn't even occur within the town limits), the planning board appropriated funds for the sign and had it installed with great pomp on the courthouse lawn in the center of our little town.

It would be more fair to innocent travelers if the sign read: *Warning, Psychological Disturbance Ahead*. But then, as I've recently begun to surmise, the world is not always fair.

Okay, I admit it, I have an attitude. However, I suspect you'd have a chip on your shoulder as well if you were my age in Bricksburg and you did not have your driver's license. That's right. I'm a seventeen-year-old guy who doesn't drive. I've been shaving for well over a year, yet when I wish to go anywhere, I must walk, ride my bike, or glom onto someone with a car. It isn't the inconvenience that bothers me; it's the shame. At my age it is humiliating arriving at a party with my mom behind the wheel. It's of little consolation that my friends all say my mom is the coolest. She may be, compared to the standard mom in Bricksburg, but that doesn't put me in the driver's seat.

I passed the written part of my driver's exam with ease. It was the driving part that foiled me. Twice. The first time I forgot to hook my seat belt, and Gene, the tester guy, failed me before I drove out of the parking lot. The second time a woman named Faye administered my test. I was doing great until parallel parking, when I clipped a truck and ripped the side-view mirror off my mother's car. Not to make excuses—it was my fault and I accept full responsibility for the accident—but I think it's only fair to mention that Faye was wearing a miniskirt she must have borrowed from a little sister and a sleeveless blouse that hugged her like wet tissue paper. Yes, I know, I should not have allowed myself to be distracted. But I did. And now, having failed the test twice, I must wait until November before I can get another learner's permit and apply to take the test over.

I am writing this in the middle of July. November is a full four months away. I hope I don't go nuts before then.

Yes, going nuts is something I worry about often. Later I will tell you about my aunt, which will partially explain my interest in the subject. However, for now, let me get on with my story. (I realize I've used the word *however* twice so far in this text. I am liable to use it many times again before I am done. I have a thing about vocabulary and become easily attached to certain words that strike my fancy. That's part of who I am.)

My best friend, Isaac, called this morning, and I agreed to meet him and his sister at Billy Goat this afternoon. Billy Goat is an old, abandoned concrete bridge a couple of miles outside of town. It spans the Itchatoni River. The original road leading to Billy Goat was bypassed about twenty years ago, and a new road and a new bridge were built. Nowadays no one uses the bridge except idle teenagers looking for a place to hang out. It's a relatively private retreat, far enough from town to keep little kids away. Another advantage to Billy Goat is that when you get bored hanging around with your friends (if you have any), you can jump into the river and float downstream.

The rear tire on my bicycle is flat and I don't feel like digging around in the shed for the air pump, so I decide to walk to Billy Goat. I walk so much it has become my trademark in town. Old folks sitting on their front porches mumble to each other as I pass by. I can't actually hear what they say, yet I imagine something like this:

"Look, Doris, the Rowe boy is walking again."

"Eh?"

"Never mind."

"Tell me. I want to know."

"I said, the Rowe boy is walking again."

"I can see that. I'm not blind."

Sometimes I feel like shouting at the old folks, "Walking is good for you. Get off your wrinkled bottoms and move." But of course, I don't shout. There are already enough crazy people in town. No need for me to behave irrationally in public.

Mom is working at her desk in her office as I prepare to leave the yard. Before departing, I yell to her through an open window, "If Ariel Crisp calls, take a message, will ya?"

"Sure, Cecil, but didn't you say Ariel was an insufferable snob?"

"I may have said that last year, but Ariel has changed a lot since her dad moved in with Trudy Benson. I think the scandal brought her down a notch. Anyway, she's having a party next weekend and I heard she was inviting people today."

"I'll take a message. Don't forget, though, you and I are going to Staunton next Saturday."

"Oh, right. To see Aunt June. We'll be back by four, won't we?"

"We should be."

"No problem, then. I'll have time to get ready. See ya."

"Be home for supper."

"Yep." I walk as far as the gate, then turn and call to Mom, "By the way, if Ariel doesn't call, I was right before. She is a snob."

Snob or no snob, Ariel Crisp is the best-looking young woman in King County. I often dream of her at night wearing a bathing suit. (She's wearing the suit. Not me. I sleep in boxer shorts.) Ariel has silky, strawberry-colored hair, greenish eyes, a pretty face, a shapely body, and a voice capable of cutting through all my defenses. If I were to go crazy tomorrow, Ariel would be largely responsible.

It's a short walk from the neighborhood where I live into the surrounding countryside. Half a mile north of town I turn east on Paige Road and start for the lowlands along the Itchatoni River. I've ambled less than a hundred yards when Virgil Spintz zooms up in his brand-new, tomato red BMW convertible. Virgil is my age, more or less. He couldn't be more conspicuous if he hired a consultant to advise him. He slows to a stop, lowers the volume on his CD player, and removes his tinted sunglasses. "Going somewhere? Want a lift?"

"Nope."

"Nope, you're not going somewhere? Or nope, you don't want a lift?"

"Both," I answer precisely.

Virgil frowns, shakes his head, and exhales loudly. "Don't tell me you're still mad about that Isaac thing. I told you before, Cecil, I never said his name."

I do my best to appear offended as I resume walking.

Virgil watches me depart, then wheels his car around in the road and screeches off in the opposite direction.

Here's what happened: About a month ago someone altered three letters in the Welcome to Historic Bricksburg sign. They used white paint to change the *i* and *o* in *Historic* to *y* and *e*, then covered the bottom loop of the *B* in *Bricksburg* with green paint that matched the background. Maybe that someone was Isaac Yardley. Or maybe it wasn't. (I don't honestly know, yet if I did, I wouldn't publish the fact in a book.) Anyhow, whoever painted the sign, the cops were predictably annoyed and swore they would snare the vandal (or vandals) before the end of summer.

Here's where Virgil Spintz fits in. About two weeks after the incident, one of Bricksburg's finest—a deputy sheriff named Harold Fassel—clocked Virgil going a hundred and ten miles an hour on the flats south of town, yet Harold did not give Virgil a ticket for speeding. Fine. I'm all for giving people a break . . . unless they turn that against you or one of your friends. Although Virgil denies that any of this happened, I'll let the facts speak for themselves. Less than an hour after not writing Virgil a ticket, Harold suddenly figures out who vandalized the welcome sign and drives directly to the Yardleys' house to arrest Isaac. Fortunately Forrest Yardley was home at the time or

Harold would've hauled Isaac straight to the police station for questioning. So far no charges have been filed; however, the crime is being relentlessly investigated and everyone knows Isaac is the primary suspect.

FACT: Isaac isn't a criminal. He may get a little rebellious from time to time, but so did George Washington, Patrick Henry, and lots of other upstanding Virginians. Rebellion and miscreancy are not the same animal. Isaac has strong convictions and is bold enough to say and do what he believes, yet he isn't mean-spirited or destructive in nature. Indeed, Isaac is probably the sanest person I know. He never compromises his beliefs for the sake of social convenience.

Billy Goat

The town of Bricksburg sits in the middle of King County, which in turn lies in the heart of a broad Tidewater region that extends south and east from the center of Virginia to the Atlantic coast and the shoals of the Chesapeake Bay. The land around here is mostly flat. It is wet with creeks, ponds, swamps, and lazy little rivers. This is snapping turtle country.

Snapping turtles have irritable dispositions. Even the babies are vicious. If you are foolish enough to taunt a snapper, it will do its ornery best to snag one of your fingers, or toes, or whatever appendage it can reach. A polite retreat is the wise course of action when encountering a snapper.

Some people claim there are cougars living deep in the swamps of King County. I've never seen one, but then, I'm not crazy; I don't frequent the backwaters. Around here all you have to do is stand in sight of a swamp and the mosquitoes come carry you away.

Twenty minutes after walking rudely away from Virgil, I veer off Paige Road onto a footpath cutting through a thicket of scrub trees. The path soon takes me to the old, forgotten lane that winds through the woods to Billy Goat Bridge. The aged pavement has long since cracked apart and deteriorated from lack of attention, and the route is overgrown with briers, bushes, and weeds. I follow the derelict trail for approximately a thousand yards and soon come to the final bend before Billy Goat.

I whistle to announce my imminent arrival. My signal is soon answered in kind, and then as I round the bend I see Isaac. He is sitting barefoot and shirtless on one of the ivy-covered walls of the bridge, drawing with colored pencils in a sketch pad that he holds on his lap. The leafy boughs of oak and elm trees leaning from the riverbank shade all but the center of the span where Isaac is situated. He greets me without looking up from his work. "Cecil. Glad you could make it."

"Yep. Thanks for calling." I halt near the foot of the bridge. "Don't let me interrupt you."

"I won't."

A moment passes. I slap an attacking mosquito. "So where's Isabel? I see her bag."

Isaac points with a pencil. "Ten o'clock on the horizon."

I lift my gaze to where Isabel is ensconced on a branch high over the river. She is sixteen, with jet black hair and big brown eyes. For most of my life I always thought of Isabel as Isaac's witty, flat-chested little sister. I can't do that anymore. She's still witty, but she has grown. When I catch her eye, she smiles and says, "Long time no see."

"Yesterday, wasn't it?" I reply with a smile of my own.

"Ah. That's sweet," Isabel coos facetiously. "You remember."

Isaac glances up at his sister and quips, "Cecil has a mind like a mudflat. Once something gets in there, it sticks."

"It's true," I agree. "I have a superb memory . . . although for the life of me, Isaac, I can't remember why we are friends."

"I wasn't aware we were."

Isabel laughs. "You set yourself up for that one, Cecil."

I sidle over to peek at Isaac's pad. It takes me a moment to appreciate what he has done. Soon, however, I realize I'm looking at a rendering of upside-down images. It's a drawing of reflections on the water. There's the underside of the bridge . . . I see trees reaching toward a patch of clear sky . . . there are Isaac's legs and torso dangling off the bridge wall.

"It's just a study," Isaac offers modestly. Then he closes his pad, sets it carefully on the stone-capped wall beside him, rises to his feet, and without pause or preamble dives into the river below. That's Isaac for you: everything in one fell swoop. I watch as he swims toward a solitary rock about forty yards downstream. The rock is smooth and flat on top. We call it the Indian Seat.

Isabel comes down from her tree and joins me on the bridge. We sit in a pool of sunlight, our backs resting against a wall. She's wearing cutoff blue jeans, a T-shirt, and a pair of brown tennis shoes. She crosses her legs, uncrosses them, then crosses them the other way. I notice they've recently been shaved. She reaches for her bag and takes out a thermos. "Ice tea?"

"Yes," I say, and spotting the tattered spine of an old book in her bag, I ask, "What are you reading now?"

Isabel and I share a passion for literature. We both love to read. She wants to be an English professor or maybe an editor when she grows up. I have vague ambitions of becoming a writer. Isabel, who rarely goes anywhere without a book, retrieves the one in her bag and says, "I'm rereading *Gulliver's Travels*. It's great. You want to hear something hilarious?"

"Sure. Shoot."

Isabel flips to a marker and explains, "This is from when Gulliver visits the Grand Academy in Lagado and meets a language professor." Then she takes a breath and begins to read: *"The first project was to shorten discourse by cutting polysyllables into one, and leaving out verbs and participles, because, in reality, all things imaginable are but nouns. The other was a scheme for entirely abolishing all words whatsoever, and this was urged as a great advantage in point of health as well as brevity. For it is plain that every word we speak is in some degree a diminution of our lungs by corrosion, and consequently contributes to the shortening of our lives. An expedient was therefore offered, that since words are only names for things, it would be more convenient for all men to carry about them such things as were necessary to express the particular business they are to discourse on."*

We both laugh as she closes the book, and I remark, "No one would ever discuss elephants if that plan was adopted."

"Did you know Jonathan Swift was kidnapped as a baby?" she asks.

"No."

"Well, he was. His nanny took him. The woman was expecting an inheritance from a cousin who was dying on an island in England and she wanted to secure her money, and so she took Jonathan with her by boat from Ireland without telling Jonathan's mother where she was going. When his mother learned where her son had gone, she sent word for the nanny not to risk another voyage until the boy was older. So the nanny kept him on the island until he was almost three years old. She must have done a good job of raising him, because when he returned to Ireland, Jonathan could count and read passages from the Bible."

"Why didn't his parents go get him?"

"Because Jonathan's father died before Jonathan was born, so he couldn't go anywhere, and I guess his mother was weird about boats. Or maybe she was just weird."

I let a few seconds pass before asking, "Did you know my dad died while Mom was pregnant with me?"

Isabel nods.

I wasn't fishing for sympathy when I asked the question, and I'm not in the mood for serious sentiment, so I make light of the matter. "Alas. Boring me. I was never kidnapped."

"No," says Isabel, "but your aunt did try to shoot you when you were a baby. That must have been character building."

I shrug. "I was three months old when that happened. I doubt it affected me at all. It's funny you should mention Aunt June, though. Mom and I are going to visit her next week."

Isabel doesn't say anything for a moment. Then she surprises me by asking, "Could I come with you?"

"Are you kidding?"

"No. I think it would be . . . interesting."

As Isabel knows, my aunt has resided in a mental hospital for most of the past seventeen years. "Interesting isn't the half of it when visiting June."

"I know, Cecil, but I'm serious. I'd like to go."

A look at Isabel tells me she is sincere, and after quick consideration, I reply, "Let me check with Mom. If it's okay with her, it's fine with me."

Isabel is clearly pleased. "Great. Just tell me when. I'll be ready."

At this point a dripping wet Isaac reappears on the bridge and gestures for Isabel and me to sit apart. "You're hogging the sun," he says in a tone that suggests we should know better. "I didn't bring a towel to dry off."

Isabel and I look at each other and roll our eyes before shifting in opposite directions. Isaac plops down between us, makes himself comfortable, and, out of the blue, announces, "I've made a decision. From now on when I'm in public, I'm going to cultivate a gruff exterior."

"Do what?"

"You know, wear a stern demeanor," Isaac answers flatly.

Isabel asks the logical question. "Why would you want to do that?"

Isaac turns his face to the sun and adopts a deep thinking expression. Isabel and I know the look well, and knowing it, we resign ourselves to waiting until he's ready to speak. In due course he sighs and says, "It's the stink around the welcome sign. Everybody already presumes that I'm the one who vandalized it, or almost everybody, and now when I go out in public, everyone stares at me as if I were some sort of hardened criminal. So I've decided to play the part and scowl angrily at anyone who looks sideways in my direction. They're expecting to see a villain and I don't want to disappoint them."

"Some redneck might get the wrong idea and come after you with a stick," I note with a laugh.

Isaac grunts. He isn't daunted.

Isabel directs a challenging smirk at her brother. "Okay, Mr. Gruff Exterior. Let's see what you've got."

Isaac pauses, then clamps his jaws tight, wrinkles his brow, narrows his eyes, and glares at us with what he imagines is a spiteful expression. Isabel and I erupt with laughter and she says, "You look constipated."

"Quick, give him a laxative."

Isaac frowns and shakes his head. "Children. There's not an ounce of gall between you. I suppose you'd rather I walk around like a guilty dog."

"Guilty is as guilty does," I point out to Isaac.

The sharp tone of his response surprises me. "Were you there? Did you see me paint the sign?"

"No. But you said—"

"I said I was out that night."

"And you said you knew who painted the sign."

"I did not," Isaac snaps tersely. "I said I thought I knew who painted the sign. There's a difference, Cecil. I didn't make a confession."

"Okay. I take your point. So who do you think painted the sign?"

Isaac grimaces and turns his face back to the sun. "I'd rather not say. It's just a hunch."

"That's a cop-out."

"I'm not copping out. I'm exercising my constitutional right to be silent."

I press no further. Isaac will tell me when he is ready to tell me, and not before. And as if to emphasize that fact, he blatantly changes the subject. "So, Cecil, are you going to Ariel's party?"

"If she invites me. You?"

Isaac grins. "Of course. It's a pool party. Ariel will be wearing a bikini. Do you think I'd miss that?"

I start to chuckle, then suppress my mirth as Isabel rises abruptly to her feet. She flashes a disgusted look at Isaac and me before crossing to the far side of the bridge.

"Don't be mad at me," I offer. "I didn't say anything."

"No, but you were thinking it, Cecil."

I consider defending myself, but decide to let the matter rest. The fact is, I am guilty as charged.

My Aunt June

As I said before, I spend a lot of time thinking about crazy people. There is nothing mysterious about this—no psychologist is needed to uncover some deeply suppressed childhood memory. My interest in the subject is clearly linked to Aunt June. The woman is clinically insane. She has papers to prove it.

Before I explain about June, I should introduce you to her younger sister, my mom. Her name is Mary. She grew up here in King County. Her life hasn't been easy. Her parents, my grandma and grandpa, moved to Florida when I was six. We see them every couple of years or so. Typical retirees, they stay busy doing nothing every day. I give them credit for one thing: They got out of Bricksburg.

Mom met my father at a dance in Richmond when she was twenty-two. By her account, Dad literally swept her off her feet. He was thirty. His name was Milton. A year after the dance they got married and he moved to Bricksburg. Although I never met the man, judging from the pictures I've seen, he was a pretty nice guy. (It may sound weird for me to say that about my progenitor, but it's true: Milton is smiling in every photograph I've seen of him.) Like me, Milton had ambitions of writing professionally. Unfortunately he never finished any of the stories he started, so it was impossible for him to earn a living that way. Instead he worked as a clerk in a building-supply store. Mom says he had beautiful hands.

When Milton went, he went all of a sudden. One evening he came home from work, complaining of a headache, and after supper he went to lie down on the couch while Mom washed the dishes. By the time she hung up her apron and went to check on him, he was gone. A vessel in his brain had burst. BOOM. The man Mom loved had entered the irretrievable past.

Two months later I popped into the world, and then, three months after my arrival, Mom's older sister, June, slipped over the proverbial dividing line and tried to blow our heads off with a shotgun. People theorize that June went mad with envy because she wasn't married and didn't have a baby of her own, but no one really knows for sure why she did what she did. June marched into the house with a double-barreled twelve-gauge, aimed in our direction, and pulled both triggers. She missed, of course, or you wouldn't be reading this story. The blast blew a hole in the wall above the couch where Mom and I were sitting. (As a matter of note, it was the same couch where Dad died. Mom got rid of it a few years later after one of our neighbor's cats peed on the cushions.) Everyone who is old enough to recall the shooting claims it was a miracle June missed from such close range.

Despite my claim at having a good memory, I do not remember anything about that near fatal day. However, I am frequently reminded of the incident whenever I sit in the living room and glance at the spot where the wall was repaired and wallpaper replaced. The more I consider the event that precipitated the repair, the more I'm convinced June intentionally raised her aim at the last instant. I know her pretty well. She can be as disoriented as a lost chicken at a crossroads, but I don't believe she would deliberately kill anyone.

To sum up Mom before turning my full focus to June: Within a five-month period Mom lost her husband, had a son, and watched her sister aim a shotgun at her face. All things considered, I'd say Mom has held up rather well. She has peculiarities, just as everyone does, yet she's a cheerful person and leads a completely functional life. If only that could be true of her sister.

According to Mom, June was always high-strung as a child, and as she got older she became increasingly agitated by little things. For example, she might scream at a door that wouldn't stay closed or cry because a broom was broken. In retrospect, Mom now understands that these were early symptoms of June's mental disorder, but at the time people just thought she was short-tempered and overly dramatic. No one grasped the extent of June's problems until after she attempted to blow our heads off and she was sent to Western State Hospital. The doctors there immediately diagnosed her as a schizophrenic.

Schizophrenia is one of the least understood of mental diseases. It is a psychotic disorder characterized by loss of contact with the environment and the disintegration of the personality. The symptoms vary from individual to individual, from one mind to the next, yet on the whole it is a chronic ailment capable of inducing much misery in the afflicted. I wouldn't say June has a mild case of the disease, yet fortunately her condition is not compounded by paranoia, which is often true with schizophrenics. Nor is June possessed by demons. Although she sometimes hears voices in her head, she reports that they are generally pretty polite. In that sense I suppose you could say my aunt June is lucky.

She has been living at Western State Hospital in Staunton, Virginia, since the summer of the shotgun incident. Western State is an insane asylum. With Grandma and Grandpa living so far away, Mom and I make an effort to visit June once every three or four months. June claims she is happy at the hospital and never wants to leave the place. That may or may not be so—June often says things just to get a reaction. Whatever; the staff at Western State tells Mom and me that June is one of the most popular patients in the institution and has many fascinating friends. I can vouch for that. I've met a few of June's friends, and they are definitely fascinating.

A couple of years ago Aunt June somehow determined that I was in training to become an astronaut, and now every time she sees me, she wants to know how I intend to entertain myself in outer space. No sense in arguing with June, so I answer that I plan to read lots of books and stare out the window. She thinks that's very sensible of me.

The last time Mom and I visited June, she gave me a drawing she'd done of the Milky Way. (The drawing is tacked on the door to my bedroom. Essentially it consists of thousands of silver dots on black paper. If I stare at it too long, I get dizzy.) On the same visit June also advised me to buy a good dictionary before going into orbit. "You'll want to be prepared in case you encounter any big words you aren't familiar with, Cecil. After all, you'll be alone up there and won't have anybody to answer your questions."

"What about extraterrestrials?" I asked, hoping to humor June.

She didn't laugh. Instead she said, "I may be crazy, but I'm not stupid. Extraterrestrials don't speak English."

June is full of astute observations, and I often get the impression that she is more sane than she lets on. What separates her from mainstream humanity is that her observations usually occur in several dimensions simultaneously. That would be an asset if she was a theoretical physicist, but she's not. She's just an individual struggling to think things through.

There's one last aspect to Aunt June that I should mention, and that is the care with which she grooms herself. I'm no expert on middle-aged people, but she seems like a rather attractive woman to me. She has a longish face with sharply pronounced cheekbones, big brown eyes, and a tall, thin, perfectly proportioned nose. June is fastidious about her image, and I cannot remember ever seeing her without her hair neatly coiffured, her makeup discreetly applied, and her clothes perfectly pressed. This impeccable presentation of self makes for an odd contrast when speaking with June. You find yourself looking at a fashionable society matron while listening to a mental patient.

Species out of Control

It's five-thirty when Isabel, Isaac, and I leave Billy Goat and walk out to Paige Road, where we say good-bye. They live in the opposite direction of town, about a mile east of the river.

Arriving home, I find Mom in a rocker on the front porch. Her feet are propped on the rail and she's reading a book called *The Future of Agriculture: How Will We Feed Ourselves in 2050?* Mom loves that sort of factual stuff. She's a history teacher at a private school in Binkerton, about twenty miles north of Bricksburg, and during her free time she's writing a book about the population explosion. An excruciatingly slow writer, she's been working on her book for the past three years. I honestly don't know where she finds the patience.

"How was your day?" she asks as I amble onto the porch and sprawl out in the hammock.

"So-so."

"See Isabel and Isaac?"

"Yep."

"Spare me the details, Cecil. I wouldn't want you to sprain your tongue."

I consider telling her about the proposal to reduce words that Gulliver heard from the professor at the Grand Academy but decide it is too much effort to explain. Instead I volunteer, "We hung out and talked."

"Oh. Sounds like loads of fun," Mom says in a mocking tone.

I lie quietly in the hammock, studying the pine ceiling and listening to the moan of Mr. Henshaw's lawn mower across the street. Two houses down, Wayne Beaman has an Orioles game on the radio. Somewhere in the distance I hear a dog yapping. It's Rufus, the dumbest canine I've ever met. He barks at everything but cats. After a while I roll onto my side in the hammock and ask Mom, "Do you think your book will be published?"

"That's the idea."

"I hope it's a best-seller and we get rich." After Mom fails to reply, I add, "Being rich would be fun."

"It would be a change." Mom has a habit of making wry understatements. Some of them are funnier than others. Many go right past me.

Mom and I have a pretty close relationship, and I mean that in a genial way. There's none of that Sigmund Freud stuff going on between us. I read his book *The Ego and the Id*, and I think the man was seriously confused about sex. He attempts to boil everything down to the Oedipus complex. In case you don't know, Oedipus was a Greek male who killed his father and married his mother. It was an accident—Oedipus didn't know who they were. Even so, that didn't stop Sigmund from basing a whole field of psychology on the incident. According to Freud, all boys growing up reach a point when, and I quote, "the boy's sexual wishes in regard to his mother become more intense and his father is perceived as an obstacle to them; from this the Oedipus complex originates. His identification with his father then takes on a hostile coloring and changes into a wish to get rid of his father in order to take his place with his mother." Did you ever hear such malarkey? Freud either had a complex of his own or he was trying to see how many people's legs he could pull.

I'll admit it, I love my mother, but don't think for a minute I want to get in bed with her. That's disgusting. I'd rather shave my head and go to school naked.

Anyhow, Mom's book is serious. The subject is us: you and me, and the rest of the exponentially expanding human population. According to her, we are a species out of control.

Anthropologists argue over the details all the time, yet there is a general consensus among them that *Homo sapiens sapiens* (the current version of humankind) evolved into existence approximately forty thousand years ago. We started as migrating, club-wielding hunters. Over time we learned to cooperate in groups, then we learned to grow crops and to speak languages and eventually we settled down in towns. Living in towns gave birth to the concept of civilization, and after becoming entrenched in that, we rapidly evolved into what we are today: a race of credit-card-carrying, hair-transplanting, moon-walking, sitcom-watching, liposuctioned idiots. (Pardon my attitude.)

However, it's not what we as a species have become that boggles the mind. It's our numbers. Ten thousand years ago there were five million, seven hundred thousand humans on the planet, which is hardly enough to populate New York City. But by the turn of the seventeenth century, the world's population had risen to one billion. By 1930 that figure had doubled to two billion. After that, things really took off. In the next thirty years the population climbed to three billion (we are worse than rabbits), and thirty years after that, in 1990, there were more than five billion humans on the planet. Barring some unforeseen cataclysmic event—such as an asteroid colliding with earth or viruses raging out of control—there will be well over six billion of us vying for our planet's resources by the year 2000.

Six billion: That's six thousand million people . . . all of us wanting breakfast and supper every day. You don't need to be a statistician to spot a trend here. There are problems on the horizon. At the rate our numbers are expanding, there won't be much room left on earth for other mammals in the year 3000, not that there will be any left. We probably will have eaten them all by then.

Maybe I exaggerate, but not by much.

Perhaps it's the result of living with someone who is writing a book about the population explosion, or maybe I'm just odd, yet I often sit out on the front porch at night, wondering how many Cecils there are in the world. As far as I know, I'm the only Cecil in King County, but there must be dozens of others living in the state of Virginia. Texas probably has hundreds of Cecils, and I wouldn't be surprised if England has thousands.

"Mom?"

"Yes, son?"

"Do you think humans will go the way of dinosaurs?"

Mom hems thoughtfully. "It's possible, in some future ice age or period of severe climatic change."

"So maybe I'm going to school for nothing?"

"Sometimes it seems that way, Cecil."

I let that remark pass and ask, "How many stars did Aunt June say there were in the Milky Way?"

"Billions."

"More than people?"

"Way more. Billions more. Why do you ask?"

"Just thinking. Do you remember what Aunt June said was going to happen in the future?"

"She says so many things."

"True, but this stuck in my mind. According to her, by the time humans completely trash the earth and exhaust all its resources, we will have built enough spaceships for everyone to move to another solar system."

"June may have a point there."

A pause ensues, during which Mr. Henshaw finishes his lawn and shuts off his mower. Rufus is still yapping in the distance. Then Mom remembers to tell me. "Oh. I nearly forgot. Ariel Crisp called and invited you to her party. She wants you to RSVP. She was very charming on the phone."

"Ariel can be sweet when she wants," I allow. "Thanks for taking the message."

"Just doing my job." Mom rises from her rocker and starts for the door. "Time for supper."

I flop sideways out of the hammock. "What's on the menu?"

"The usual. Fried lizard guts and baked prunes."

"Yummy. I'll do the dishes."

Self-Conscious

I wait until two o'clock on Sunday before calling Ariel. Although I am only RSVPing to her party and have nothing to be nervous about, I feel a twinge of apprehension as I dial her number. Actually, what I feel is more than a twinge. Indeed, I'm beset by a mild case of the jitters. What causes this? Fear of rejection? Or excitement at the prospect of hearing the voice that goes with the person I desire? This romantic attraction stuff is curious. It has a peculiar way of making little things large.

Ariel's mother, Claudia, answers on the third ring. She sounds as if she has just woken up. "What can I do for you?" she asks when I give her my name.

"I'd like to speak with Ariel about her party."

"Hold on while I find her."

Now I remember hearing that Claudia Crisp hasn't been able to sleep much at night since her husband left home and that some doctor wrote her a prescription for antidepressants. I bet that's why her voice sounds so funny.

"Yell-o."

"Hi, Ariel. It's me."

"Cecil?"

"Yep. I'm calling to put my name down for your party."

"You're down," Ariel says matter-of-factly. "Here's the scoop. We start in the pool at five, so bring a bathing suit. Then it's a barbecue from seven to eight, and afterwards the Land Sharks will play until eleven-thirty."

"You got the Land Sharks!"

"They only charge two hundred dollars," Ariel replies with counterpoint calm. "Dad's paying them."

"The Land Sharks are hot. Sounds like a fun party."

"Wouldn't be a party without fun."

"You're right there," I agree. "So Ariel . . . you going to the softball games tomorrow night?"

"I haven't decided. Are you?"

"Nothing else happening."

"Maybe I'll see you there. I have to go now, Cecil. Grace Cullighan is here helping me organize stuff."

"Oh. Say hey for me."

"Will do. Bye."

After putting down the receiver, I stare for a while at my reflection in the hallway mirror. I'm slender, five foot eight-and-a-half inches tall, with pale blue eyes and mousy brown hair. Some days I almost believe that I'm handsome—not too handsome—just pleasant to look at. It mostly depends on my hair. I never know how it's going to behave. My hair has a rambunctious mind of its own.

Softball is a big deal in Bricksburg. Without softball in the summertime, eighty-five percent of the people in this part of the world would not have a social life. Unless a tornado is on the horizon or it's raining hard enough to drown a worm, there is a league that plays in the field behind the high school each Monday and Wednesday night throughout June, July, and August. There are eight teams in the league. Four of them play on Monday. Four on Wednesday. Three of the teams have only black players, three are lily white, and the remaining two are racially mixed. The rosters more or less reflect the statistics and cultural attitudes in King County. I'm not going to make any apologies for this less than perfect ideal; that's just the way it is around here. However, on the playing field there are no complaints. Oh, there are a few angry exceptions to the rule—black and white—but they rarely come to the games. They've learned. No one has any tolerance for politics or social dissension on softball nights.

The fans are wildly enthusiastic, and there are lots of them. When all the players on all the teams bring their wives or girl-friends, their children, cousins, and next-door neighbors—which many of them frequently do—you have a substantial crowd on hand. Add ex-wives, independent sports fans, lonely people, and bored teenagers, then the stands on both sides of the field are filled well beyond their intended capacity.

I arrive at the field after the start of the first game on Monday night and see Pauley Harrington leaning against the fence near the concession stand. I'm fond of Pauley. He's a straight-up guy with no pretensions. However, Pauley's family raises chickens, and due to the mildly insistent aroma of manure that accompanies Pauley everywhere he goes his social status is relatively low.

He doesn't actually smell as bad as people like to pretend. I think he deserves more credit than he gets. As I head in his direction I notice that he is looking rather glum. "Hey, Pauley. What's happening?"

He hesitates before replying, "Maybe you can tell me. I saw Isaac a few minutes ago and he gave me the creepiest look. It was like he thought I turned him in to the cops or something. You know I wouldn't do that."

"Of course not," I say with alacrity. "And anyhow, Isaac doesn't think you squealed on him. That was him experimenting with a gruff exterior."

"Excuse me?"

"It's not worth explaining. But you can trust me on this, Pauley. Isaac doesn't blame you. I'd know if he did."

Pauley is visibly relieved.

"So where'd you see Isaac?"

Pauley jerks a thumb over his shoulder. "Out in front of the school, standing next to Grace Cullighan's car."

My inclination is to split right away, yet I don't want to abandon Pauley too abruptly, so I ask about his missing dog. "Any sign of Bravo?"

Pauley gives me a sore look. "No. Not yet."

I immediately regret my inquiry. I was just trying to show Pauley a little friendly concern. Instead I've hit him where he is already bruised. There's nothing for me to do now but make the best of my gaffe. "Hang in there," I offer philosophically. "I'm sure Bravo will come home eventually."

Pauley looks doubtful. "Maybe."

"He will," I say. "Be cool. I'll see ya."

"Yeah. You too."

Upon exiting the fenced-in area around the playing field, I see Grace's big, black Buick parked in front of the high school. Lucky Grace. She inherited the car from her grandfather. Isaac is standing on the driver's side of the vehicle, speaking to Grace, and Gary Perkins is on the other side, speaking to someone in the passenger seat. As I continue my approach I realize that someone is Ariel Crisp. She is slumped down in the seat, probably trying to get away from Gary, who is no doubt holding forth about his intended move to Hollywood. I wish the guy would pack his bags and get going already.

For reasons that I do not fully understand, yet I suspect are linked to Ariel's presence, my mind takes an unwelcome turn as I approach the car. It jumps into a freeze-frame mode, and for a hypersensitive moment everything appears clipped and divided, as if I'm viewing snapshots of my friends. Then Isaac sees me coming and breaks the spell. He calls my name and starts around the car to meet me. Ariel lifts her gaze and observes me in the side-view mirror. Gary turns and nods nonchalantly. Grace flings open her door and hops out to follow Isaac.

Good old gregarious Grace. She leaps across the ditch to the bank on which I'm standing and kisses me on the cheek. She and Isaac are a couple, although they have a very loose relationship and people often wonder what is going on between them. Grace is blond and blue eyed. She isn't glamorously beautiful like Ariel, yet she's pretty in a clean, healthy sort of way. A talented amateur photographer, Grace has only one flaw that I am aware of: She doesn't know how to laugh. When she is amused, she shrieks, squeaks, and squeals.

Grace, Isaac, and I sit on the grassy bank beside the car. Ariel rises up in her seat, reaches through the open window, and moves Gary out of her line of vision. Her long, silky hair is gathered loosely atop her head in an unruly bun. She fixes her greenish eyes on me and smiles. "So, Cecil, I want to hear about your big date."

I am perplexed. And I show it.

Ariel blows an errant strand of hair from the tip of her nose and laughs. "Don't be shy. We're all friends here. You can tell us."

I hear Isaac moan. Gary is looking very smug.

When I speak, my voice doesn't behave quite properly. "What date? What are you talking about, Ariel?"

Ariel just looks at me and continues to smile. Then Grace brings me up to speed. "She's talking about Isabel, Cecil. We heard you were taking her to meet your aunt this weekend."

"Sorry, Cecil, I mentioned it earlier," Isaac confesses.

My temperature rises and I begin to blush. (I hate when that happens.) "Isabel asked to go, so I said yes. I hadn't thought of it as a date. It's no big deal."

Ariel gives me a look that is hard to read. On the surface it appears a little sad, as if she's hurt that I've decided to date Isabel, but I sense mockery lurking beneath her expression. After a moment she bats her lashes at me and declares, "I think Isabel is sweet. I just hope you aren't late for my party."

"I'll be there."

Grace diverts the attention away from me by slapping at a mosquito and cursing like a mechanic. (Cursing like a mechanic is an acquired talent. Her father and her uncle own a garage in town, and Grace learned how to curse before entering kindergarten.) Everyone laughs at Grace's outburst and laughs again when Isaac remarks that he isn't fond of mosquitoes either. And then, just when I'm beginning to escape the shackles of self-consciousness and relax, Ariel gives Grace a look and pulls the plug on our gathering. "We'll be late if we don't get going."

Going where? Late for what?

Grace rises to her feet. Isaac and I follow suit. She kisses him quickly on the lips, pats my shoulder good-bye, and returns to the car. Grace starts the engine. Ariel waves. The Buick glides off. Afterward Isaac and I exchange adieus with Gary, then head toward the ball diamond.

As Isaac and I walk away I see Gary walking to his car on the far side of the road. It seems unlikely, yet I have a nagging hunch that he's going somewhere to rendezvous with Ariel and Grace. But then Isaac puts my mind at ease. "Ariel and Grace are having dessert at the Greasy Spoon with Ariel's dad. He's been acting extremely weird lately."

"Weird? Like how?"

"I don't know, but Ariel is worried about him."

"Oh. Speaking of worried, Isaac, I saw Pauley Harrington earlier and he was worried that you think he fingered you to the cops."

"Wonder why he thinks that."

I laugh. "Well, he said you slammed him with a pretty nasty look."

Isaac winces. "Guess I did. Poor Pauley. I'll apologize if we see him. By the way, I'm eighty-sixing my criminal persona. It doesn't work."

"Imagine that."

Isaac shrugs. "It was just an experiment. Say, do you know, did Bravo come home yet?"

"He's still missing."

Bravo

Tat-a-tat. Tat-a-tat.

I awake on Tuesday morning to the patter of rain hitting the roof. It's a soothing, hypnotic sound, and if it wasn't necessary to get up and pee, I'd let myself drift right back to dreamland. Yet duty calls, so I rise and head toward the bathroom. Vaguely, in the back of my mind, I recall having dreamed about Pauley Harrington's dog, Bravo.

I return to bed and prop myself up with pillows. Except for the dog, I can't remember anything about the dream.

Pauley lives with his parents and three brothers. The Harringtons are a close-knit bunch. Until earlier this summer they had a dog named Bravo. They all loved him very much. I suppose they still do.

Bravo is a midsized, rust-colored mutt with a long, collie-style nose. The tip of his left ear is missing and his tail shows signs of having been broken on numerous occasions. One cannot fairly describe the dog as handsome, yet there is an aura of dignity about Bravo that lends to his attractiveness. Like any good dog, he harbors a wide variety of prejudices. To name a few examples: Bravo hates kites, motorcycles, red cars, and wheelbarrows.

One day Pauley's oldest brother, Michael, was returning home on his bicycle when he saw Bravo in a field cavorting with a fox. Michael watched in amazement as the animals circled each other, kicking up their hind legs, tumbling and twisting acrobatically. It was obvious to Michael that Bravo and the fox were playing a game, although he could not make out the rules or the objective of their game. He watched the two animals for several minutes until finally the fox suddenly caught wind of him and skedaddled. The alert carnivore knew precisely how many chickens it had snatched from the Harringtons' henhouses.

When Michael reached home, he ran excitedly from Harrington to Harrington, describing what he had just seen.

That night at dinner Mr. Harrington informed his family that Bravo would have to be quarantined for six weeks while they watched him for signs of rabies. All four brothers immediately began to protest their father's cruel decree, but then they withdrew their objections when Mr. Harrington explained the only alternative. Putting Bravo to sleep simply was not an acceptable option.

All right, said the brothers, Bravo isn't going to approve of this, but we'll fix up a stall for him in the barn and take turns visiting him night and day.

The Harrington boys were good to their word. Regularly for the next six weeks, for at least twenty minutes an hour, every hour from seven in the morning until ten-thirty at night, Bravo was attended by a family member.

Pauley told me that sitting in the barn with Bravo was one of the hardest things he'd ever done. By his account, Bravo could talk, or rather he could string together a series of guttural whines and whimpers that sounded like someone talking. After a week or so in his pen, Bravo began to plead for his own release. "Why are you doing this to me?" he would ask whichever brother was sitting with him. "I've been loyal since I was a puppy. I thought you loved me."

The Harrington boys would try to explain to Bravo that they were penning him up for his own good, but he refused to listen to reason and continued to berate them daily.

Throughout the forty-two-day incarceration period Bravo never foamed at the mouth, nor lost his balance, nor demonstrated any symptoms of a viral infection. Finally, with the whole family watching expectantly, Mr. Harrington entered the pen, inspected the dog's gums and eyes, and determined that he did not have rabies. Cheers rang out when Mr. Harrington ordered Bravo's prompt release. The gate to the stall was thrown open and Bravo was invited to the house for sausages.

Bravo did not move. For one long, solid minute he just glared at the Harringtons, one by one. Then he shook his head in bitter disappointment, exited the pen, and walked slowly past the family without sparing anyone a parting glance. He entered the barn lot, slipped under a fence, trotted across the adjoining field, and disappeared into the far woods. That was the last glimpse the Harringtons had of their dog.

Tat-tat-tat. The rain continues to fall on the roof above my head while I continue to think about Bravo. The writer in me, or rather the part of me that wants to one day mature into a writer, senses a deep significance in Bravo's story. In many ways it qualifies as a morality tale, especially when you consider that Bravo did not understand the word *quarantine*. In his mind the Harringtons crossed a critical line when they took away his freedom. All noble dogs require freedom of movement, and if Bravo was to keep his spirit and self-respect, he could not forgive even his loved ones for locking him in the barn for six weeks. That was akin to tearing out his heart.

Poor Bravo. Brave Bravo. An honorable dog if there ever was one.

Tat-a-tat. Tat-a-tat-tat-tat . . .

Trouble

I must've fallen asleep again while thinking about Bravo, because I'm later reawakened by a knock at the door. I sit up and rub my eyes. It's still raining. "Yes?"

Mom pokes her head in the room. "Hate to disturb the dead, but you might want to get dressed. Isaac is here to see you."

"Send him in."

I hop from bed, step into a pair of jeans, and am smell testing a pair of socks when Isaac wanders in, his hair and shirt wet with rain. I can see right away that something is bothering him. "What?"

"Let me sit down," he replies, moving across the room to take the only available chair.

I pull on the socks I'm holding, slip a T-shirt over my head, and go to sit down on my bed.

He catches my eye, shakes his head, and exhales loudly. "At eight-thirty this morning Sheriff Moore and Deputy Fassel showed up at my house with a summons for me to appear in court on August fourth. Judge Steele wants to hear what I know about the welcome sign."

Although I've been expecting something like this to happen and am not entirely shocked by the news, I am slightly rattled and don't know what to say. But Isaac is looking at me with a pitiful expression on his face, so I must say something. "What's the charge?" I ask.

"Nothing yet. It's only a summons . . . but they're claiming it cost seven hundred dollars to repaint the sign, and anything over five hundred dollars is a felony. If they charge me, it will be for destruction of public property."

"August fourth," I muse. "That's two weeks away."

"Thirteen days," Isaac corrects me.

I try to keep calm. The last thing Isaac needs right now is a hysterical friend. He needs to know I am at his service, that my considerable mental resources are focused on his problem. I hem thoughtfully (I hope reassuringly) and say, "I suppose your next step is to find a good lawyer."

"No," Isaac counters. "I'm not getting a lawyer. I haven't been arrested yet, but if it comes to that, I'll defend myself. After all, I'm innocent."

I sound a dubious note. "Are you innocent?"

He frowns. "You don't believe me?"

I pause before replying. Isaac is essentially an honest person, and yet . . . well, he has an ironic streak in him and it isn't always apparent when he is joking. But then, this is no laughing matter, and the look in his eyes persuades me that he is telling the truth. "You didn't do it, did you?"

Isaac's head moves from side to side.

"Who did?"

He hesitates. "We've been through this before."

I become suddenly annoyed with Isaac and I say to him sharply, "Listen, you're my best friend. I want to help you, but I can't if I don't know the facts. What exactly is your point in keeping secrets?"

Isaac moans, an air of weary resignation about him. "My point is this, Cecil. If I tell you who I think painted the sign, when you see him, you'll look at him strangely—even if you try not to, and since everyone knows we're tight, he'll know that you suspect him, which will clue him that I suspect him. And I don't want him knowing that. Not yet. I want to see how he reacts when he hears I might be going to jail."

"Hmm. It's your call."

"That's right."

"Well, whatever happens, just tell me how I can help."

Isaac gives me a sly look. "You could start by sallying down to the police station and confessing to the crime."

I muster a wan smile. It's nice to see Isaac hasn't lost his sense of humor.

He has his mother's car and I have money, so I offer to buy him lunch at Tiny's Diner. (My grandma Rowe, whom I hardly know, has been sending me twenty-five bucks a week since my father, her son, passed away. Most of it has gone into the local bank, but I always keep a little cash on hand.) Tiny's is a rinky-dink diner out past the stoplight on Route 22. Just about everyone but Tiny refers to the place as the Greasy Spoon. On the ride over there Isaac tells me that his parents are being cool about his summons. I guess they know their son well enough to believe him when he says he's innocent.

We beat the noon rush and grab a booth by the window. Margo brings us menus. She's an interesting character. A year ago she weighed over two hundred pounds, but thanks to a strict diet of amphetamines, cottage cheese, lettuce, and pears, she lost half her bulk in the amazingly brief period of six months. She used to plant herself behind the counter and shout at customers "What ya want?" but now she glides around the joint like an Olympic figure skater. (She even wears those short skirts that skaters favor.) Tiny has been after Margo to marry him since she dropped under a hundred and sixty pounds, but so far her answer has been no. If there's any truth to the rumors, Margo has been having too much fun lately to consider the binding vows of marriage.

She's always been fond of Isaac. "Sorry to hear about your troubles," she says to him as she skids to a halt by our booth. "If you decide to split town and need money for a bus ticket, you come to me, you hear? I've got a hundred tucked away with your name on it."

"That's very generous of you, Margo," Isaac says politely. "But I'm not going anywhere. Tell me, though, how'd you know I had trouble? I only found out this morning."

Margo seems caught off guard by Isaac's question. The lines around her eyes suddenly tighten, and she touches nervously at her permed hair. A brief moment passes before she answers with a laugh, "This is the Greasy Spoon. If something happens in King County or is about to happen, the announcements are posted here."

Isaac nods. "So the word is out, huh?"

"I reckon it is," Margo allows, tapping her check pad with a pen. "Now, what are you boys having?"

We order turkey platters, an iced tea, and a Coke. As Margo glides away, Isaac whispers across the booth, "That was odd. I got the impression she knows something."

"Me too," I concur. "Her face actually twitched."

By twelve o'clock the Spoon is packed, and as I look around it is obvious that everyone either knows about Isaac's summons or is currently hearing the news. It's also obvious that Isaac's logic of withholding information from me is flawed. When anyone glances toward our booth, I stare back, wondering if I am looking at the culprit who vandalized the welcome sign. On the other hand, maybe there is wisdom in Isaac's logic, for it isn't long before I suspect everyone in the diner . . . which effectively means I don't have a clue.

Isaac and I are shoveling turkey into our mouths when Gary Perkins appears in the doorway with an umbrella hooked over an arm. A voice in my head shouts that Gary is a perfect candidate for the crime. I watch Isaac's eyes for clues, but they give no hint that Gary is the guilty party.

Gary wanders over to say hi. I don't know why I let him bother me as much as he does. He's a decent guy—he's never done me wrong—but there is something about the way he presents himself that strikes me as superficial, and I always feel a little false after talking with him. Perhaps I'm jealous of his relationship with Ariel. I'm not too proud to admit that possibility.

"Gentlemen," Gary says with a casual nod. "Just heard about your summons, Isaac. What a bummer."

"Yeah, it's a drag."

"A guy can't get away with anything in this town. That's one reason I'm moving to LA."

That hits a raw nerve with me, and before I can stop myself, I remark, "I hear you can get away with murder there."

Gary gives me a perturbed look. "I'm not sure what you mean by that, Cecil."

I feel suddenly remiss. He's done it again. He's drawn me into pettiness. "I didn't mean anything," I apologize. "I guess I'm just a little uptight right now . . . after what happened to Isaac and all."

Gary assumes the high moral ground. "I understand, Cecil. We're all upset."

"What are you guys upset about?" asks Isaac. "I'm the one headed to the guillotine."

"Let them eat cake," Gary quips theatrically. (Those actor types are always looking for opportunities to ply their trade.)

Isaac and I laugh. Credit where credit is due: It was a funny thing to say. Also humorous is the way Gary spins on his heels and lurches for a stool at the counter that a customer is in the act of vacating. "I'm going to grab that sucker while it's warm," he says as he departs.

Isaac waits until Gary is out of hearing distance before muttering, "With his wavy hair and that little nose of his, Gary sort of looks like Marie Antoinette."

I snort, shooting cold soda through my nose. Ow. That hurts.

It's still raining when we leave the diner and head toward my house so Isaac can drop me off. He has to have his mother's car back by one. As we wait for the green at the stoplight I ask Isaac, "Are you or are you not worried about your summons?"

"I don't look worried?"

"No. You don't seem to be sweating it at all."

The light turns and we get up to cruising speed before Isaac replies, "Yes, I'm concerned. Don't think I'm not. But knowing I'm innocent helps take the edge off things."

"What if you're falsely convicted?"

Isaac shrugs at that. "I'd deal with that knowing the truth would come out eventually."

"Maybe I could speed up the process if you told me who you think painted the sign."

"Use your imagination, Cecil. How many people in Bricksburg have enough gumption to paint the welcome sign? Or rather, how many of them have enough wit to alter the letters the way they did? Those three little blobs of paint changed the whole meaning of the sign. To do that required smarts."

"Well, then it must have been someone from out of town."

Isaac grins. We turn on Hickory Street and drive to my house. I hesitate before hopping out of the car. "Seriously, how come you're so cool about the situation you're in?"

Isaac narrows his eyes in thought, then gives me the type of answer that only he among my friends can come up with. "Life is short. The way I figure, if you're not making the most of it, you should at least be making the best of it. In this situation, keeping cool is making the best of it."

"That simple, huh?"

"It works for me."

I hop out of the car. "Billy Goat tomorrow?"

"If it ever stops raining."

Walking Fool

After Isaac drives off, I linger on the porch for a while, watching rainwater drip from a hole in the gutter. I promised Mom I'd fix that leak, but it will have to wait. I'm not going up on a ladder today. Even if I didn't fall and break my neck, the tar wouldn't adhere properly to the wet metal.

I go in to find Mom and tell her what happened to Isaac, but she's asleep on the couch in her office, her nose literally in a book. The screen on her computer pulsates with stars zooming past central perspective. (Is that what astronauts see when whirling through space?) I scribble a note and stick it on her computer. *Caught you napping. Gone for a walk. C.*

There is nowhere to go. I just walk. My nose leads. One foot follows the other. I love walking in the rain. Somehow it strengthens my small thoughts and gives clarity to ideas that usually float away in dry weather. Maybe I have a low-barometer mind.

The rain has suspended all foot traffic in Bricksburg, and I feel as though I'm walking through an old, familiar, black-and-white photograph. There's the brick Baptist church on my left. The brick Methodist church is on my right. Not far ahead is the brick Presbyterian church, right beside the brick doctor's office. Then there's the courthouse and the jail. Yes, they are made of brick. If nothing else, this podunk I call home was built to last.

I pause at the Welcome to Historic Bricksburg sign. A beer bottle and a lollipop wrapper litter the nearby ground. If I squint and look real hard, I can just barely discern where the altered letters were repainted. A felony charge for that? Seems like a lot of trumped-up flapdoodle to me.

Walking, walking. I continue past the high school, past the Frosty Treat ice-cream parlor, past the Gulf station . . . on toward the road to Sparta.

Sometimes I wonder if I have a nervous disorder or if the way I think and feel are normal by-products of being seventeen. I frequently worry about things that do not exist, unless thoughts and abstract notions are things. Whatever. The fact is, I often grow anxious about nothing.

I was explaining my worry-about-nothing tendencies to Isabel the other day and she quoted Hamlet, or rather Shakespeare. He wrote: "There is nothing either good or bad, but thinking makes it so." That reminded me of Freud, who wrote: "The ego is the seat of anxiety." These statements are no doubt true—they have a neat elegance on paper—yet they do little to alleviate my tendencies. What am I supposed to do? Surrender my ego and quit thinking altogether? Fat chance. I'd just be no one worrying about nothing.

The rain diminishes to a steady drizzle as I proceed past the turnoff to Sparta and start along the flats south of town. The road here runs straight for several miles through marshy low-lands and is sometimes witness to an unusual phenomenon. If it has been raining like today, and then the sun breaks through to heat the moist pavement, thousands of little frogs hop out of their boggy homes and sit in the steamy mists that rise from the road. Unfortunately this is a suicidal activity for many of the frogs. When drivers attempt to swerve and miss one frog, they usually wind up mushing another.

As I walk, my mind drifts back to last night's encounter with Ariel Crisp. She was toying with me, poking fun at my weak spots, and I just sat there like a vulnerable child. I really must learn to protect myself better, although I suppose I should be thankful Ariel is not a malicious person. Her games are only games. She doesn't torture the losers.

She and I kissed at Virgil Spintz's party last April. We were slow dancing to Sade when she surprised me with her open mouth. (Ariel, not Sade.) It took me a second to get over the shock, but then I started kissing back with all the sensitivity I could muster. I must have done okay, because we continued making out for more than a minute and did not part lips until the song was over. I wanted to keep holding her and maybe snuggle a bit, but then someone put on a fast song and we danced apart like everyone else. After the song was over, Ariel flitted off and I couldn't find her for the remainder of the night. I kept my cool when I went looking for her. (I didn't rush around calling her name or anything desperate like that.) How-ever, I was persistent and did venture into every room in the Spintzes' huge house before abandoning my search and going home. If Ariel was still there when I left, she must have been hiding in a closet, and I didn't think it was proper to go snooping in the Spintzes' closets.

The hardest part was waiting to see Ariel again. Thirty-two hours passed before that happened in the hallway at school on Monday morning. I admit, I was a bit worked up by then and probably exuded intensity, but hey, I'm a guy and I had tasted her lips and was anxious to stake a claim on kissing them again. I can see now in hindsight that I was caught up in my own desires and not thinking rationally about Ariel, who is a masterful tease if there ever was one. I'm not sure what I was expecting from her, but it certainly wasn't the cool reception I received. She pretended that nothing had happened between us. "Hi, Cecil," she said as she fiddled with her hair. "Great party the other night. See ya. I'm in a rush. I can't be late for Covington's class again."

"Oh," I replied, my ego shattering into shards and falling on the floor around me.

"God, I hate algebra," she remarked over her shoulder as she walked away.

Witty me. "I don't like algebra either," I muttered as I watched her depart.

Since then it's been a little of this and a little of that with Ariel, most of it impossible to interpret. I've tried repeatedly to forget that we kissed and shake her out of my head, yet she has an amazing instinct for knowing just when to flatter me with attention and reassert herself in my mind. It's spooky, really. Sometimes I think she must be psychic.

I emerge from my ruminations and note that I am now less

than a mile from the Harringtons' farm. I stop on the side of the road for a moment and consider whether to pay Pauley a visit or turn around and retrace my steps to town. As I stand there in the rain, in limbo, I see the speck of a car in the distance. It's a red speck, which grows larger and is soon identifiable as Virgil Spintz's BMW.

Well, I'm not going to hide in the woods, so I wait where I am. As Virgil draws near I lift a hand and wave. It's not a signal for him to stop. I'm just saying hello.

Virgil stops. The automatic, driver's-side window goes down and he studies me with a look of curious concern. "What are you doing out here in the rain?"

"Nothing."

Virgil grins and shakes his head. "Want a ride?"

I shrug. "Do I deserve one? I was pretty rude the last time you offered. Besides, I'll get your seat all wet."

Virgil reaches into the rear seat and grabs a sweatshirt. "You can sit on this."

I mumble thanks as I get in the car and am immediately intrigued by the handsome arrangement of gauges mounted on the dashboard. Those Germans sure know how to manufacture a luxury vehicle.

"Where to?"

"Town, I guess. I wasn't going anywhere."

As we approach the turnoff to Sparta, Virgil asks, "In the mood for cruising some back roads?"

What the heck. "Sure. Let's ride."

Virgil downshifts and whips the BMW into the turn. We travel silently for several minutes, then he says, "Today is Tuesday, Cecil. I've got something I want to show you."

"What?"

"I'll show you when we get there."

"Fine." I shrug. "But what's Tuesday got to do with it?"

Virgil gives me a cryptic little smile. "What I want to show you is only there on Tuesdays and Wednesdays."

It's All Relative

Virgil's dad owns an oil and gas distributorship and is probably the second-richest person in King County. (Top financial honor goes to Ariel's father, Randolph, who works as an equities analyst.) As Virgil and I glide safely along the winding wet road I ponder the cost of owning and driving a high-performance vehicle such as his. I'm not crass enough to ask how much his dad paid for the car, but I figure it would run a minimum of thirty grand to purchase and insure the car. Maybe more.

I'm no pauper. Thanks to seventeen years of Grandma Rowe's monthly checks, to my mother's fiduciary discipline, and to compound interest at the bank, I have almost nineteen thousand dollars to my name. That seems an immense amount of money to me, although there are people in this world who would view it as an insignificant sum. After all, there are bond traders on Wall Street who occasionally earn nineteen thousand dollars in a week, and a few select athletes are paid more than twice that much for playing a single game.

Yes, a game.

Everything is relative. Mom told me that according to the United Nations, the poorest one billion people on earth cannot afford to purchase a sufficient amount of calories to grow and develop properly. That is an astounding statistic. Humans can get all the calories they need from beans and basic grains, yet if the United Nations report is accurate (I imagine it is), there are one thousand million people on earth too poor to buy these essential commodities at market price. Forget fruit, forget vegetables, milk, meat, cookies, pie, and all other nutritional niceties westerners take for granted. Forget everything you think you know about going hungry and consider this: The best that one out of every six humans on earth can reasonably hope to eat in a day is a small bowl of gruel and maybe a little bread. Think about that the next time you whine because you can't have chocolate on your ice cream after dinner.

I don't know what a billion hungry people looks like, but I'm sure it's not pretty. Now, consider that while a billion people struggle to survive each day on cold cereal, there are doctors in this prosperous nation of ours accruing personal fortunes by removing cosmetic fat from patients who are simply unhappy with the way their bathing suits fit. *Sad* is the word that comes to mind.

Before leaving this tangent and returning to the rainy day in King County that Virgil picked me up on the side of the road, it would be only honest of me to confess: I feel bad about the billion starving people on earth, yet at the same time I covet this luxury car I'm riding in and wish I had one of my own. Maybe not a red one, although I'd take whatever was available.

Sparta makes Bricksburg look like a sprawling metropolis. It is a speck on the map, consisting of a post office, a store with a gas pump, and seven farmhouses. Soon after Virgil and I zip through the hamlet, I ask him idly, "What are you going to do after high school?"

"Go to college."

"What for?"

"Girls."

"I mean, what will you study?"

"Philosophy."

That surprises me, and I tell Virgil, "I had you pegged for a business major."

"You had me wrong, Cecil," Virgil says without emotion, then adds in explanation, "It may be because I've grown up with the stuff, but I'm not really interested in money. I certainly don't want to spend my life thinking about profit margins. How about you? What will you study?"

I shrug. "If I go to college, which I suspect I will, I'll probably study literature. I think fiction is in my blood."

Virgil surprises me by saying, "My dad told me your dad wanted to be a writer."

"Your dad?"

"He was talking about growing up in Bricksburg and I asked if he knew your dad. He said, 'Yeah, pretty well.' "

I acknowledge Virgil with a nod and slip into a reflective silence. For me, my father has always been an abstract idea . . . a sort of friendly spirit that exists in the story of my past, and it now feels strange to hear him mentioned as someone that other people actually knew. Of course, it makes sense that Milton had friends; I just never thought of him as a social being. Freud wrote, "I cannot think of any need in childhood as strong as the need for a father's protection." If that is indeed the truth, I spent my childhood protected by a ghost.

We are about three miles west of Sparta when Virgil whips off the paved road without warning and turns onto a small, well-maintained dirt road. He drives about a hundred yards to the crest of a wooded knoll and stops near a break in the trees. To the right is an old split-rail fence covered with honeysuckle. Virgil switches off the engine and reaches for his door handle. "We're here," he announces.

There are not many hills in King County that afford sweeping views of the land, yet the knoll on which we now stand in the drizzling rain is an exception. We lean against the fence, looking east across a gently rolling pasture with a creek running through it. There are cows in the pasture, which is encircled by a barbed-wire fence. Beyond the fence is a small ranch house, and beyond that a vast field of corn. The corn looks healthy. The house has seen better days.

After taking in the view I turn to Virgil with a questioning look. He gestures for me to study the scene again, so I do, and after a moment he asks, "What do you see behind the house?"

"A shed and three-quarters of a green pickup truck."

"Hold on a second." Virgil goes to the car and reaches into the glove box. He returns with a pair of binoculars. "Take a good look at the pickup and tell me if you've ever seen it before."

It takes me a moment to focus the lenses. "Let's see, now . . . that's a Ford. Is it the one Harold Fassel drives when he's off duty?"

"Bingo."

I lower the binoculars and gaze at Virgil. "This isn't where Harold lives, is it?"

"Nope."

"Okay, Virgil . . . you going to tell me what you're thinking, or do I have to guess?"

Virgil enjoys a little laugh before replying, "That's Margo Clay's house. Tuesdays and Wednesdays are her days off from the Greasy Spoon."

I peer through the binoculars again. I'm starting to get the picture. "Harold got married, didn't he?"

"Yep, to Bridget Taylor. Nothing meek about her."

"Hmm. So Harold is making time with Margo. That is very, very interesting."

"I thought it might fire your imagination, and I bet Isaac would be fascinated as well."

"What are you thinking now?"

Virgil doesn't smile, not exactly, yet there's a hint of amusement in his voice when he answers, "I was thinking Isaac might want a photograph of Harold coming out of Margo's house."

"Blackmail?"

"I prefer to think of it as a bargaining chip," Virgil says with a completely straight face. "It sounds more civilized."

"Grace," I mumble. "She's got telephoto lenses."

Virgil nods. "I figured she did."

I eye Virgil with growing respect. I'm now almost certain that he painted the welcome sign, and yet, appreciating his not wanting to take the blame, I have to admire his effort to get Isaac off the hook.

"Come on." Virgil gives me a comradely pat on the shoulder

before turning on his heels and starting for the car. "Let's get out of here before someone happens by."

On the ride back to town I consider asking Virgil if he'll let me drive for a while, but I ultimately dismiss the notion. I don't want him to feel as though I am trying to take advantage of our newly emergent friendship.

The Untold Universe

After Virgil drops me at home I run inside to call Isaac, but he's out, so I leave a message with his mother for him to call me back. I hate waiting for people to return my calls. For some reason, time seems to stretch out while I wait, and I grow anxious worrying about nothing. Did something go wrong? Did the person receive my message and decide to ignore it? The more time that passes, the more I fret. The more I fret, the more ridiculous I feel. Is this a modern phenomenon, a new kind of telephone anxiety? Or is it merely old-fashioned uneasiness?

The phone rings just as Mom and I sit down to eat. It's Isaac. I alert him that I have important news and say I will call back as soon as dinner is done. Twenty minutes later when I pick up the phone and dial the Yardleys' number, I get a busy signal, which suggests they are now having supper. (Isaac's father always takes the receiver off the hook before the family sits down to their evening meal. Forrest Yardley has been interrupted by phone solicitors one too many times.) I help Mom with the dishes, then dial the number again. Isabel answers and we exchange hellos. When I ask to speak with her brother, she says he left the house five minutes ago.

"What?" I blurt, then continue heatedly, "He wasn't supposed to leave. I told him I had important news."

Isabel sighs patiently. "Sorry, Cecil."

"No, I'm sorry," I tell her. "It's not your fault."

"Has your news got anything to do with Virgil Spintz?"

"Why? Did Isaac go somewhere with Virgil?"

"I think so," Isabel allows, then explains, "Virgil called about ten minutes before you did, and that's who Isaac said he was going to meet when he borrowed Mom's car."

I groan. A moment ago I was the fleet-footed messenger with late-breaking news, but now I'm just a guy peddling yesterday's headlines. On top of that, I feel like the third man out. Why didn't Isaac call me first? Why wasn't I invited to this powwow?

"You still there?"

"Yeah."

"Want to tell me what's going on?"

"I'm not sure anything is *going on*," I say flatly. "But Virgil may have information relating to Isaac's summons. More than that, I should leave it to Isaac to say."

"Fine. Keep your secrets."

"I'm not keeping secrets . . . I'm just being discreet."

"Okay. Guess who called me this morning and invited me to her party."

"Must have been Ariel," I say in a sinking tone, painfully aware that Ariel called Isabel the day after teasing me about our supposed date. Suddenly I'm a guy with old news who feels ignored by his best friend and socially duped by the redheaded object of his desire. "Are you going?"

"I plan to, depending on whether we visit your aunt June or not and when we get back if we do."

"Oh, right. Mom says she'd be delighted if you came with us. We'll be home in plenty of time for the party."

"Fantastic. I like your mom. What time should I be ready?"

"Nine o'clock. We'll pick you up. Now, Isabel—I don't know what you're expecting—but Aunt June can be a real challenge. She's got a funny habit of asking embarrassing questions. And not just one, but three or four questions on a string."

"I've got nothing to hide."

"If you do, she'll find it. Whatever happens, you'll have a day to remember."

"Good. I like memorable days."

"Famous last words. So, maybe I'll see you tomorrow at Billy Goat. When Isaac gets back, don't forget to tell him I called."

"I won't."

After hanging up the phone I muse for a few moments in the hallway mirror. Sometimes I don't understand myself at all. What is this melancholy that has suddenly come over me? So what if Isaac went to meet Virgil and Ariel invited Isabel to her party? Big deal. I can't expect everyone to clear their plans with me before they act. I don't rule the world. Is my ego so delicate it must take everything personally? Of course, that's what egos do—they take things personally—but that's not my point.

I nod farewell to my reflection in the mirror and begin the task of distracting myself while waiting for Isaac's call. I try the tube, but nothing interesting is going on there, so I flick it off and complain to Mom that I'm bored. She says that isn't her problem and suggests I read a book. That's the thing about moms. The good ones are always out to improve your character.

I've read everything in my library, so I venture into Mom's office and peruse her shelves. *The Untold Universe*, by Krol Zandinski, catches my eye and I pull it down. Hmm. Perhaps I'll glean a few bits of intergalactic knowledge before my upcoming visit with Aunt June. I lug the book into the living room and ensconce myself in the easy chair that Mom won in a rescue squad raffle. It's an ugly piece of furniture, but comfortable and well lit by an overhead lamp.

I soon learn that I'm sitting approximately one hundred million miles from the sun. Ten thousand miles is difficult for me to fathom, and I'm utterly lost when it comes to grasping one hundred million. The best I can do is imagine a great distance and tell myself I have not imagined far enough.

The more I read, the more astounded I become. This cosmology stuff is huge.

According to Krol, the universe consists of billions and trillions of miles of vast nothingness. It is practically void of substance. In other words, for the amount of space that exists, there is very little matter to fill it—imagine a pea sitting in an empty ocean basin, with many trillions of miles lying between each basin. For example, the nearest star to our sun, Alpha Centauri, is twenty-five trillion miles away. Wow, you gasp (or at least I did), yet in the overall scheme of the universe twenty-five trillion miles hardly constitutes a skip and a jump. It translates into about four light-years, which is merely one twenty-fifth of the width across the galaxy we live in, the Milky Way. Now hold on to your hat—the Milky Way is only one of a hundred billion galaxies, all of which are trillions of miles apart from one another. Our sun, that small star that holds our solar system in place and gives it life, is but one of more than one hundred billion stars in the Milky Way.

How can I, with my puny mind, be expected to comprehend such magnified knowledge? Indeed, how can anyone? As Zandinski informs his readers: Albert Einstein said imagination was more important than knowledge when attempting to perceive the full spectrum of reality.

I am relieved when the phone rings and I have an excuse to close *The Untold Universe*. I lay the startling book on the floor as one might set down a smoking gun and head toward the beckoning instrument.

"Hey, Cecil."

"Hi, Isaac. So, how'd it go with Virgil? He give you the scoop on Harold Fassel?"

"He did. And I already spoke to Grace. We're going to try to be there in the morning when Harold shows up. If he shows up. I'd love to get a snap of Margo meeting him at the door."

"He was there today," I note before asking, "What's the plan? You and Grace and Virgil get there early and find somewhere to wait with the camera?"

"That's it," Isaac confirms. "I haven't seen the setup yet, but Virgil says there are a few trees by the creek where we can hide. You've seen the place. What do you think?"

"You'll be all right once you get in position. The problem will be crossing from the fence to the trees. You'll be in the open for about a hundred yards."

"Hmm. I guess that's a chance we'll have to take."

I pause an instant. "You won't be needing extra bodies, will you?"

"Not really."

"Oh."

Isaac hears the disappointment in my voice, realizes I'm feeling unwanted, and is good enough to offer, "You can come if you want to, Cecil, but we're going to be risking it as it is."

"No, three is already a crowd. You guys go ahead. This is espionage. It's not a party."

"I knew you'd understand," Isaac says appreciatively, relieved that I didn't take him up on his offer. "We'll meet at Billy Goat when we're done. If Harold shows up early, we might be there by noon."

"I'll be waiting."

Stop, River; Stop, Mind

I awake at the crack of nine-thirty on Wednesday morning and am out of bed by ten. The sun is shining bright. It's a perfect day for taking long-range photographs or for fixing a leaky gutter. After eating, I zip to the hardware store and purchase a can of roofing tar from Billy Compton. By a quarter to eleven I'm on the ladder, patching the gutter.

The patch job takes fifteen minutes, plus an additional half hour to clean the tar off my hands. (I lost my concentration for one second and grabbed the wrong end of the putty knife.) Soap is useless on tar, so I resort to gasoline, which does the trick but burns like the dickens where I cut my finger. Oh, well, the dickens aren't too bad. At least I didn't fall off the ladder and break my neck.

I slap together two cheese sandwiches on rye, put them in my side bag with a notebook and a pen, and start walking. I expect I'll have to wait a while before Isaac shows up and figure I might want to use that time writing. Writing what, I don't know, but the tools will be available if I think of something. At ten past noon I've arrived at Billy Goat Bridge and taken up a shaded perch on the south-facing wall.

At twelve-thirty I'm still waiting, so I pull out my writing implements and stare at them blankly for several minutes. If I'm going to grow up and write novels, I ought to begin sharpening my word usage skills. But how? What do I say? Hmm. Do I just pick up the pen and put it to paper? No, that doesn't work. Think some more. Got it! Describe what you are seeing and feeling, make it pleasing to read, and try to be interesting.

Here goes: "The river flows like time beneath my dangling feet. In the distance I hear a duck quack. Quack. Meanwhile the Itchatoni gurgles merrily along. The mind is like the river. It thinks and thinks and never stops. Damn thing. One wrong turn and it carries you into a swamp. That's how people go crazy. The river deposits them in a quagmire and they can't get out. There's the duck again. Quack."

My pen takes a rest and my thoughts flow to a farm near Sparta where my friends are busy without me. The events of today will surely become a prominent chapter in King County's cultural history. For generations to come people will tell the glorious story of how Grace Cullighan, Isaac Yardley, and Virgil Spintz induced Harold Fassel to drop his investigation into the welcome sign case. But Cecil Rowe was absent and his name will not be mentioned.

Again I take up my pen. "The mind is an unruly bear. Petty emotions are its claws. Instead of gloating over who gets credit for what, I should be hoping my friends obtain a revealing photograph. Yet what do I do? I sit here whining for attention. My ego is more dangerous than a bear, for it's an irrepressible creature that never hibernates. Compliment me, it clamors. Feed me, it screams. Put Cecil at the center of the world."

"Cecil."

I jump at the sudden sound of my own name and just barely avoid falling from the wall. After steadying myself, I whirl around and bark, "Isabel! You didn't whistle."

"Sorry, my mind was elsewhere. I saw a chipmunk."

"A chipmunk. Isabel, I nearly fell in the water."

She just smiles, drops her bag on the bridge, and hops onto the wall beside me. She's wearing blue-jean shorts, a T-shirt with Daisy Duck emblazoned on the front, and flip-flops. Daisy is wearing a miniskirt and drinking a martini. Isabel glances at my open notebook. "Whatcha writing?"

"Nothing." I close the notebook and set it to my left, away from Isabel. She gives me a look that says you-must-have-been-writing-something. I ignore her look and inquire if Isaac has come home yet.

"No," she answers in a clipped tone. Isabel is miffed because no one will tell her what Isaac and Virgil are doing.

I play the innocent outsider. "Hey, they didn't invite me to go with them."

Isabel is not fooled. She knows I know and she says so with her eyes. I shrug and volunteer part of what I know. "Virgil found out something about Harold Fassel that might help Isaac."

Isabel turns her gaze downriver and pauses a moment before asking, "Did you know Virgil asked me out?"

I pause a moment myself. "When?"

"A couple of weeks ago."

I'm glad Isabel isn't watching my face. Her answer has disturbed me more than I would care to admit. "What did you tell him?"

Isabel cuts a quick look in my direction, then returns her eyes to the river. "I said, 'Thanks for asking. I'm flattered, but I kind of have my eye on someone else.' Virgil was cool about it. He didn't pressure me or anything."

"Virgil has manners," I mutter, but that's a superficial response. My emotions are churning beneath the surface, and they aren't making butter. I have been caught by surprise . . . by my own feelings. They don't approve of Isabel on a date with Virgil. I tell myself it's none of my business what Isabel does with whom. She's not my girlfriend. I have no claim on her independence. But those are just words. They do not calm my inner turmoil. Although Isabel said no to Virgil on this past occasion, that does not ensure she would turn him down again. Yet what do I do? I mean, I have a pretty good hunch as to who Isabel kind of has her eye on. Has she just rolled the ball into my court? Am I supposed to say something? What?

I like Isabel. We have much in common. She's pretty, smart, and good for me. Nevertheless, I hold back from her . . . all because of my irrational desire for Ariel, whom I can hardly trust and certainly cannot depend on. Even if Ariel and I did get it together romantically, she'd just tie me up in knots and swing me around like a rope. Still, I continue to want Ariel, and my wanting throws up a wall between Isabel and me. Or at least that's the way I explain it to myself. Maybe it's just an excuse for keeping Isabel at bay . . . for not leaning over right now and kissing her on the lips. I bet she'd let me if I tried. She has a generous mouth. Her lips are nice and full.

"Cecil."

"Yes?"

"Remember we were talking about your mom's book and you said a major problem with the population was that people were living longer than ever before, that the old folks weren't dying fast enough to make room for the babies?"

I'm relieved by the change of subject. "I remember. Why do you ask?"

"Well, I was thinking about it last night when I was reading *Gulliver's Travels* and he met some struldbruggs."

"Met some who?"

"Struldbruggs, the immortal citizens of Luggnagg. Luggnagg was one of the last places Gulliver visited on his way home."

"Oh."

"Only a few immortals were born in each generation. You could tell a child was going to be one if it had a red dot over its left eye. Anyway, since they never died, there were several thousand of them in Luggnagg by the time Gulliver arrived."

"People who live forever. That's just the sort of thing that would horrify Mom."

"The normal Luggnaggians were horrified as well," Isabel replies. "They despised the immortals. At first Gulliver was fascinated with them and presumed they were superior beings. But he revised his opinion after learning that all struldbruggs were peevish, morose, vain, dead to affection, and incapable of friendship."

"I suppose eternity is hard to bear."

"Especially if you are dead to affection."

In the pause that follows I ponder a fact that Mom recently told me. She said by the year 2000 there will be more than a quarter of a million U.S. citizens over the age of one hundred. That's twenty times as many centenarians in the population as there were a mere fifty years ago. Obviously, average life expectancies are on the rise. And what with all the recent advancements in medical science, who knows? A century from now the notion of struldbruggs may not seem so far-fetched as it did when *Gulliver's Travels* was first published.

Out of the corner of my eye I watch Isabel rise and stand on the wall. She kicks off her flip-flops, strips to the bathing suit she has on under her clothes, and bunches her dark hair into an elastic tie that she takes from her wrist. Like her brother, she's slender, somewhat lanky, with well-defined leg muscles, a flat stomach, and a long neck. But there the similarities stop, for Isabel has gently curved hips, firm, fist-sized breasts, and small, rounded shoulders. She looks down, catches me studying her figure, and says with a wink, "Watch this."

So I watch as she springs from the wall, spreads her arms, holds her legs together, points her toes, and arches her back in a swan dive. Sploop. She hardly makes a splash as she slices into the water. I applaud when her head pops above the surface. She smiles, turns in the water, and swims toward the Indian Seat.

Alone again on the bridge, I reach over and pick up my notebook. I don't open it. I just hold it in my hands and wonder if I have what it takes to succeed as a writer. Academically, I am barely average on a good day, and as for demonstrated abilities, all I've ever written are a few mushy poems, the botched beginnings of some corny short stories, and numerous sketches such as the one I was writing before Isabel arrived. Hmm. Not much evidence there. And then there's the unpublished ghost of my father. That doesn't bode very well for my prospects.

However, I'm a teenager and it's my duty to have impractical dreams. I'm supposed to follow my heart. I am permitted to heed my own urges . . . even if they make no sense and I don't completely understand what is behind them.

Earlier in this century there was a writer named Somerset Maugham who thought he was dying of a terminal illness and decided to put everything he knew about life in a single book. He called it *The Summing Up*. In it he said this about writers: "We do not write because we want to; we write because we must."

Must is a powerful word. It's an urge transformed into a need. I don't feel that strongly about writing. Not yet. Nevertheless, I think I know what Somerset was saying. He was talking about consuming passion, which is akin to having an incurable disease that doesn't go away until you do.

Incidentally, the man was wrong about his illness and lived many productive years after completing *The Summing Up*.

I put my notebook back down on the wall, look downstream, and see a mermaid lying on the Indian Seat. Her hair is spread out on the rock like a fan. In a flash I realize that Virgil has little to do with my confused feelings about Isabel. It's not him that bothers me specifically—it's the concept of Isabel dating in general. Some guy might take her somewhere, be real sweet for a couple of hours, and then try to kiss her. And she might let him. It could happen.

Agh. Stop it, Cecil.

Stop, river. Stop, mind.

Where is Isaac? It must be two o'clock by now. I'm tired of wondering what happened in Sparta. I'm tired of feeling left out of the club. I'm tired of sitting here on Billy Goat Bridge, jumping through mental hoops.

It's time to act. I yank off my shirt, kick off my shoes, hop onto the wall, and leap.

CANNONBALL.

Ow. That hurts worse than blowing soda through my nose.

Mad Cow

Isabel and I are on the wall, eating cheese sandwiches, when we hear the sound of Isaac whistling. I reply with a whip-poorwill call, which is answered by a couple of whistles that are not familiar to me. I look at Isabel. She doesn't recognize them either. We drop from the wall and walk to the west end of the bridge. Soon Isaac emerges into view, followed closely by Grace and Virgil.

"How'd it go?" I call impatiently across the distance.

Isaac rolls his eyes as if to say you-are-not-going-to-believe-this and is preparing to answer when Grace emits an amused shriek and declares, "Isaac is dangerously ignorant about cows. 'Don't worry, Grace,' he kept telling me. 'Angus are a gentle breed. They never charge.'"

Isaac shakes his head at Grace. "No. I said they *almost* never charge. How was I supposed to know you were going to go pet that calf?"

Virgil looks askance at Grace and Isaac, then says to Isabel and me, "Grace ought to go out for the track team. I've never seen anyone move faster."

Isaac laughs and slaps Virgil on the back. "The way you cleared that fence, you should go out for high jumping."

Virgil laughs too. "Just trying to catch up with you guys."

My curiosity gets the best of me and I shout, "Will someone please tell me what happened?"

"Grace tried to pet a baby cow and its mother chased us out of the field," Isaac answers.

"Over a barbed-wire fence and right into Margo Clay's side yard," adds Virgil.

"It was hilarious," Grace cries. "When Margo came outside, she was bent over with laughter."

"Margo caught you?" I ask.

"Red-handed," says Virgil.

"She'd been watching from a window the whole time," Grace informs me. "She said she saw us scramble down the hill and hide in the trees."

"You talked to Margo?"

"Yep."

"She invited us in for cookies."

"It was surreal, Cecil. You should have been there. She has a huge collection of salt and pepper shakers in her kitchen."

"Rooster and hen shakers, and little baby chickens. She must have a thousand of them."

"Fascinating," I say sarcastically. "I'll have to go and see them someday. And what about Harold? It doesn't sound like you got any pictures of him."

"Nope," says Isaac. "Harold never showed up."

Then Grace informs me, "But after we talked, Margo promised she'd try to convince Harold of Isaac's innocence. She told us he already has some doubts about who painted the sign."

Isabel, who has been quiet until now, drops from the wall and says with a straight face, "I don't know what you guys were up to. In fact, I don't really care. But I would like to know, were all the shakers full of salt and pepper?"

Grace thinks that is hilarious and begins to squeak, squeal, and prance about on the bridge. Suddenly she cries, "Oh no. I'm going to pee in my pants."

"Please don't do that," Isaac beseeches her. "Not in front of my friends."

Grace screeches and flees to the woods.

As I watch Grace run it occurs to me that I no longer have to worry about being left out of a legendary chapter in King County's cultural history. From what I've just heard, it would seem the events of today might best be preserved in a vaudeville script.

"Oh, Cecil, guess what," says Isaac. "Margo may have seen Bravo. She asked what the Harringtons' dog looked like and then told us she'd recently seen a brown mutt with part of an ear missing."

"What about the tail? Was it broken?"

"She didn't say."

I hem and rub my chin.

Then Virgil offers, "If it was Bravo, he may be living somewhere in Sparta. Margo said she'd seen the dog several times."

Isaac reaches to put a hand on my shoulder. "Cecil, you're friendly with Pauley. Maybe you should give him a call and tell him what Margo said."

"I'll do that," I agree, watching as Virgil moves over to where Isabel is leaning against the guard wall and greets her with a knowing look. They exchange smiles. I cannot help but notice that Isabel seems entirely at ease in Virgil's presence. Indeed, she appears to welcome his company.

Grace returns from the woods and informs everyone that it is time for a group photograph. That elicits a few groans and some good-humored grumbling, but no one actually resists. Let's be honest: Who really disapproves of having their picture taken?

Grace, who is after an arty effect, assumes the role of a movie director and starts telling each of us where to stand. She sits Isabel on the wall, facing downriver. Virgil is sent to stand at the far end of the bridge. Isaac is ordered to stay where he is, and I'm told to squat in the middle of the lane.

While Grace is checking her light meter and fiddling with the lens, Virgil hollers forward to me, "So, Cecil, there's a strange twist in all this."

"What?" I ask over my shoulder.

"Isaac thought I was the one who painted the welcome sign, and the whole time I was thinking he did it."

I turn to Isaac, who nods and is about to add to Virgil's statement when Grace cuts him off. "Come now, children," she chides us all. "It won't hurt to be still for a minute. Cecil, turn your head."

Click.

"Hold it right there."

Click.

"No one move. I want to get a different angle."

As Grace moves across the lane I attempt ventriloquism.

"If it wasn't you, Isaac, and it wasn't Virgil, then who painted the sign?"

Isaac replies through clenched teeth. "That is now the one-million-dollar question."

Click.

"Only a million?"

"Cecil, can't you quit talking for a single second?"

Heart-to-Heart

On Wednesday night, feeling desperate with boredom and trapped without a driver's license in this rinky-dink burg that constitutes my hometown, I walk to the ballpark to see what's going on. I arrive during the second inning of the first game and luckily find room to sit on the front row of the bleachers on the third-base side of the field. Eddie Gingrich is beside me. He's a big fellow, the only guy I know who wears camouflage pants and camouflage shirts in summertime. We exchange respectful nods, then I turn to scan the crowd for members of my social clique. My search proves futile. (Our clique is not that large to begin with; we are a select group of knuckleheads.) Isaac said he might come tonight, but he stressed the word *might*. I'm not expecting him. Nor Isabel. She never comes to the softball games. Another person I know won't be here is Pauley Harrington. I called him earlier and passed on Margo's information about a possible Bravo sighting. Surely by now Pauley and his brothers are scouring the countryside around Sparta. I hope calling him wasn't a mistake. I'd hate to think I participated in creating false hope for the Harringtons. They've suffered enough already without interference from me.

The first game proceeds without much drama until the fifth inning, when Wiley Welds, the first baseman for the Hard Knockers, steps up to the plate with three men on and hits a grand slam over the center field fence. I jump to my feet and join half the crowd in cheering wildly. It's fun screaming as loud as you can and being taken for normal. Anyhow, that's what I'm doing when I feel a tug at my shirtsleeve. As I turn, Ariel catches my eye and motions for me to come to where she is standing. After gesturing she steps back and waits. She knows I will obey her command. Her confidence is not misplaced.

"I'm so glad I saw you, Cecil," she greets me with warmth. "I don't know anyone here."

I look around and smile. "Ariel, you know everybody."

"Anyone to talk to, I mean."

I hesitate. I can see now that Ariel is not her usual self. There's a strange tension in her face, and I get the impression she may have been crying earlier. "We can talk."

Much to my approval and delight, Ariel slips her left hand under my right arm and—in full view of the crowd—turns toward the exit. "Let's stroll around the high school, Cecil. I feel the need for a heart-to-heart with someone I can trust."

A quiver in her voice alerts me to the seriousness of the situation. I attempt to offer reassurance. "You can trust me. My heart is all ears."

Ariel either smiles or winces—it's hard to tell which—and says, "Cecil, you're one of the most reliable friends I have."

I've never thought of myself as reliable before, but it's a good image and I make no effort to contradict Ariel. It might upset her. Just now she's in need of support.

With Ariel still clutching my arm we cross the front lawn of the high school and continue around to the wide stone entrance steps. We sit with our backs to the school, facing a recently cut hayfield. Beyond the field the orange ball of the sun flirts with the tips of distant treetops. Neither of us speaks for a moment . . . then Ariel clears her throat and announces in a shaky voice, "Things are pretty strange at home, Cecil. It's starting to stress me out big time."

I don't know what to say, so I just shrug and wait for her to go on.

"Mom's a complete wreck. She's so depressed, she can't concentrate on anything. And Dad . . . he keeps getting weirder and weirder."

"I'm sorry to hear that."

Suddenly Ariel's expression shifts and her face tenses with anger. "I don't know what game he's playing, but it's not fair to Mom and me. In the last couple of weeks he's taken to calling in the middle of the night and pretending to be someone else."

A pause ensues, and I'm curious, so I ask, "Who does your dad pretend to be?"

Ariel shudders a little before answering, "Twice he said he was a pollster taking a survey on the war between the sexes. Mom knew it was him, but he kept denying it and insisting she answer his questions. She didn't, though, and I was proud of her for refusing. Then last night he called and said he was a traveling pharmacist. He wanted to know if anyone in our house was in the market for some discount prescriptions."

I give Ariel a sympathetic look.

She smiles to let me know that she appreciates my concern, then exhales loudly through her nose, bends forward, and covers her face with her hands. I have an urge to reach my arm around her and comfort her with a hug, yet I hesitate, afraid she might misinterpret my move. Suddenly she drops her hands, sits erect, and says forcefully, "Something alien has gotten into Dad. He was never like this before. I swear, Cecil, it's like he's been brainwashed by that tramp he's living with. I know he still loves Mom. . . ."

A silence follows and it seems to need filling, so I offer, "Love is good. I mean, it's better than nothing." Regretting my choice of words the instant they leave my mouth, I blush and look away. I couldn't have sounded more trite and shallow if I tried.

Fortunately Ariel ignores my gaffe, and my embarrassment, and moves on to her next thought. It's an angry one, delivered in a vehement tone of voice. "Some people say you're not supposed to blame the other woman. Bah. Trudy Benson is a conniving, greedy creature who wears gross amounts of makeup and doesn't care about anybody's feelings but her own."

At that moment, as if to accent Ariel's statement, I hear the crackling sound of an electrical surge as someone flicks on the lights around the playing field behind us. I turn to see if Ariel noticed the coincidence but am unable to catch her eye. She is now glaring out across the hayfield, biting her bottom lip, her brow furrowed in anger. My first thought as I study her profile is that I'm glad she's not mad at me . . . but then I glimpse something fragile and frightened in her face, and I wonder if she is on the verge of an emotional breakdown. Instinct tells me to keep her talking, and common sense advises me to leave the subject of Trudy Benson behind. So I ask, "What about your mom? Does she still love your dad?"

Ariel's expression softens as she collects her thoughts before answering. She begins with a heavy sigh, and I sense tension draining from her body. "Yes, she loves him. They've been married for twenty years and that's all she knows how to do . . . and that's her problem. It's sad. With Dad out of the house Mom doesn't know what in the world to do with her feelings; she hasn't a clue about where to direct them." Ariel pauses and sighs again, then adds in a weary voice, "I just hope he comes home before it's too late. He's hurting Mom in ways that she can't defend herself against."

I'm no doctor, but I am an amateur psychologist, and it seems to me from what Ariel has been saying that her dad is a prime candidate for professional help. I try to be delicate. "You know about my aunt, Ariel. Well, because of her I've met a few shrinks in my day, and they tell me that chemistry has a lot to do with mental disorders. I'm not comparing your father with my aunt or anything, but perhaps he should consult a psychiatrist."

Ariel grimaces. "I suggested that the last time I saw Dad, but he just laughed and told me he wasn't crazy. He said he was merely exercising his right to feel young and foolish and was just trying to rejuvenate his juices . . . whatever that means."

"Sounds like a midlife crisis to me."

Ariel cocks her head and stares searchingly into my eyes for several seconds before speaking. "I hope it's that simple, and thank you for listening to me rag about my life. I'm sorry for boring you with all this ugliness."

"I'm not bored. Besides, you have good reason to be upset. I'd probably be a mess if I were in your shoes."

A small laugh rises from Ariel. It's offered at my expense, but I don't mind. At least she isn't crying.

"Ariel . . . if there's anything I can do . . ."

"You already have, Cecil. Honestly, I feel much better now."

"Who knows, maybe things will work themselves out. They do that sometimes."

Ariel arches her eyebrows as if to say *maybe*, then reaches to touch my hand. It's a light touch, not meant for holding. "If you don't mind, let's keep everything we said tonight private."

"Sure. Absolutely. It's not my style to gossip."

Suddenly Ariel leans over and busses me on the lips. Like her earlier touch, the kiss is bestowed lightly. "Cecil, we're a lot closer now, you and me," Ariel declares as she withdraws. "That's what a good heart-to-heart does for people."

She's right, of course. I've gained some insight into who she is and what she's dealing with, and in that sense we are closer, yet it was her heart that did all the talking while mine listened, and it seems to me we're only closer in one direction. Even so I'm happy to have lent her an attentive ear and earned some goodwill points as a reliable friend. "Anytime, Ariel. I hope you know you can call on me."

"I do and I will," she says pertly, rising to her feet and extending a hand for me to join her. As I stand she takes my arm again and gives it a little squeeze. "Walk me to my car?"

"Gladly," I say, and glad is how I feel as we descend the steps and start around the school. I'm not jumping to any conclusions, but Ariel did kiss me on the lips a few seconds ago. That signifies some degree of progress in our relations. I think. Or maybe it's just another example of her uncanny knack for knowing when to reel me in. A brief three or four hours ago I was anguishing over Isabel's future affections, but now Ariel has tightened the slack on her line and pulled me back toward her net. Please, bear with me on this fishing metaphor, yet at the moment that's how Ariel makes me feel—like I'm floundering for her lure. I don't know how else to express it.

"What are you thinking?"

I'm surprised by her question and not inclined to answer it truthfully. I hesitate just long enough to think of a diverting reply. "May I ask you a favor?"

"I suspect I owe you one. Go ahead."

"Well . . . it's not my party, so excuse me if I'm out of place, but I was wondering if you would invite Pauley Harrington."

Ariel doesn't say anything until we reach her car. It's a VW Rabbit. She stops by the driver's door and pulls a set of keys from a hip pocket. "I could invite Pauley, if that's important to you."

I try to explain. "Pauley's been having a hard time lately. And I'm not just talking about Bravo running off. I think he's more sensitive than most people think. Pauley, I mean. Not Bravo. Anyhow, it would mean a lot to Pauley if he was invited."

"You really are a thoughtful person, Cecil," Ariel says as she opens her door. "You call Pauley and tell him I said he was invited."

"Thanks."

Ariel shrugs. "You want a ride somewhere? I'll drive you home if you want."

Now I shrug. "Naw. I think I'll walk."

"Thanks again for listening. See you soon."

"Yeah, see ya."

Ariel starts her car, winks in my direction, then drives away.

A Reprieve

I awake in a sweat on Thursday morning. The air is dense and humid, and hot enough to melt butter. I glance at the clock. It's nine-thirty. Even by the muggy standards of summertime in Virginia, it's early in the day for such sweltering conditions.

Like the torpid air, I do not stir. I remain on my back and stare at the ceiling. I was up late last night reading *The Untold Universe*, and many of the notions in the book continue to astound and confound me. One particularly perplexing idea was presented in a quote from Albert Einstein. He said: "The distinction between past, present, and future is only an illusion, even if a stubborn one." I wonder, Is that true? Is the passing of time merely an illusion? Hmph. If anyone I know had said that, I'd scoff. However, one can't very easily dismiss Einstein. After all, he did win a Nobel Prize for physics. He must have had some calculations to back up his claim.

Let us rationally consider: If the past, present, and future have only illusory distinctions between them, then why am I lying here in a pool of sweat? That wasn't so yesterday, and it certainly wasn't the case last January. Obviously the atmospheric conditions have changed. Did they do so instantaneously? No. That would have come as a shock to everyone in Bricksburg. It would have made the news. Thus time must have elapsed as the changes occurred. It was cold. Then it was warm. Now it is hot. Clearly that is a distinction, and there—I've proved it—Einstein was mistaken when he said what he did about time. He probably had a lot on his mind that day. Maybe *he* was suffering an illusion.

It's so hot this morning, I wonder if the earth has wobbled out of orbit and drifted closer to the sun. It could happen. According to Zandinski, the universe exists in a state of gaseous flux that is anything but stable. In theory, all the stars and all the matter stuck in their gravitational fields are currently in the process of exploding outward from some abstract center of the universe that long ago experienced a cosmic bang. I'm glad to know that; it gives me one more thing to worry about when there is nothing else to do.

I put on shorts and go sit on the front porch steps. Mom is in her office with the door closed. Earlier this morning she single-handedly dragged the air conditioner up from the basement and installed it in the window. She might have woken me up and asked for assistance, but she didn't bother. I suspect she feels guilty for commandeering the only air conditioner we own.

I stew in my sweat for half an hour, then mosey inside and call Pauley Harrington. When his mother answers the phone, I can guess from the tone of her voice that Bravo is still missing. The sad fact is confirmed when Pauley picks up and greets me with a glum-sounding hello.

I do my best to sound upbeat. "Pauley. How ya doing, man? Hot over your way?"

"About a hundred," Pauley says flatly. "How's town?"

"Stifling. So I called because last night I was—"

Pauley cuts me off before I can finish my sentence. *"Last night.* Don't remind me. My brothers and I searched Sparta from one end to the other. If Bravo was down there, he made a point of hiding when he saw us coming."

"I'm sorry to hear that."

Pauley groans. "Ahhh. Hell. I can't blame Bravo, after what we did to him."

"Pauley," I practically shout. "It's not your fault the dog ran away. Quit kicking yourself."

If agitated pauses can travel over telephone wires, that is what happens now. Pauley does not want my counsel. "So why'd you call?"

"To invite you to Ariel Crisp's party this Saturday. She says your name is on the guest list."

"Really?" Pauley sounds doubtful.

"Yes, really. Do you think I'd make up something like that?"

"I guess not. I'm just surprised, that's all. Ariel has never been very nice to me."

"She's okay once you get to know her. Anyway, the party starts in the swimming pool at five. Afterward we eat, and then the Land Sharks are playing."

"Well, then . . . ," says Pauley, a cheerful resonance sneaking into his voice. "If I'm invited, I'll come."

"Good. Don't forget a change of clean clothes for after the pool. I'll bring some cologne we can share."

"What kind?"

"Old Spice or something. I don't know."

"My brother has Brut. I'll bring that. So . . . you want a ride? I could pick you up."

I pause to consider. I could ask Isaac to fetch me or get Mom to drive me, but then Pauley would have to go solo . . . and, well, I am responsible for him going in the first place. "Sure." I accept his offer. "Swing by around five on Saturday?"

"You got it."

I smile as I hang up the phone. That's one good deed for the day. Pauley was a lot happier when he got off the phone than he was when he answered. Now for my reward, I think I'll go say good morning to Mom and enjoy a blast of cool air. I'm within a step of the office door when the phone goes *brrring*.

"Rowe residence."

"Why don't you say hello like a normal person?"

"Hey, Isaac."

"What are you doing?"

"Taking a sauna. How about you?"

"Nothing now. I was working on a painting of a cow chasing Grace over a fence, but I gave up. The cow kept looking like a sick buffalo, and Grace didn't turn out very well either."

I chuckle. "Hard working in this heat, huh?"

"Impossible. I'm coming over."

"When?"

"Shortly."

"I'll be on the porch."

Shortly for Isaac does not mean *promptly*, which is fine with me. I don't get agitated waiting on him like I do with other people. That's probably because Isaac is generally forgiving of other people's small faults and tends not to gripe about petty matters. He saves his complaints for larger transgressions. I was flattered last night when Ariel said I was a reliable friend, but I suspect that was her way of implying that she can depend on me to respond to her in a predictable manner. Anyhow, when I think of the word *reliable*, Isaac comes to mind. With him, there is a code of understanding that does not change from day to day, from circumstance to circumstance, and the theme of his personality is constant. Put simply, he is the same friend on Tuesday as he is on Friday. Now don't get me wrong, Isaac is flexible and open-minded—he's not boring—but unlike most people (myself included), he knows what he believes and his outlook on the world is stable. *Integrity* is a good word for him.

Isaac arrives in due course and sits down beside me on the stoop. He's hardly gotten comfortable when Harold Fassel drives past the house and looks over to where we're sitting. Harold proceeds to the end of the block, makes a U-turn, drives back to the house, stops, and gets out of his car.

"What's this?" Isaac mumbles as Harold steps through the gate, his shiny black shoes flashing in the sunlight.

I don't say a word. I've always thought of Harold as a tubby fellow, but as he approaches us now I see that much of his bulk is taut with muscle.

"Gentlemen," Harold greets us with a tip of his broad-brimmed hat. When I start to rise, he gestures for me to remain seated. "Stay as you are, Cecil. We won't be going anywhere. I'm here for a chat."

"Oh, I'm glad you could join us," Isaac offers in a sassy, almost snide tone of voice. I guess the heat is getting to him like everyone else. "We were just commenting how everybody's corn is wilting in this sultry weather."

I throw a critical glance at Isaac. Although he doesn't register my look, Harold does, and he says, "That's okay, Cecil. I'm not offended by sarcasm. It goes with the territory. We cops can't afford to take things personally."

Isaac gazes directly into Harold's eyes. The look on his face states clearly that he will not be intimidated. Harold doesn't flinch. (I suppose in the course of his duties Harold has dealt with tougher characters than Isaac.) They stare silently at each other for a moment, then Harold takes a handkerchief from his hip pocket and wipes his sweaty brow. As he does so, I study the pistol in the holster at his side. It's a big one. Nervousness soon compels me to speak. "Excuse me, Mr. Fassel. May we help you with something?"

"Perhaps." Harold folds his handkerchief and stuffs it back in his hip pocket. He stretches a leg, props a foot on the bottom step, rests a hand on his thigh, leans forward, and says to Isaac in an evenly controlled voice, "I hear you and some of your gang recently paid a visit to a friend of mine."

Isaac shrugs.

Harold continues in a deliberate tone. "Officially, I have no complaints about who you visit, as long as you don't harass anyone. That's officially." Harold removes his foot from the step and draws himself erect. "But this is an unofficial chat we're having right now, and in that capacity I want you to know I won't tolerate you snooping where you don't belong. I have no idea what you were hoping to achieve, but what goes on in my private life is none of your business. Do you copy?"

"I copy," Isaac answers in a neutral tone. He may have his convictions, but he's not stupid. He knows the difference between being intimidated and asking for trouble.

"Good. Now copy this. I don't approve of gossip about my private life. We don't want any unfounded rumors going around."

Isaac cracks a thin smile. "No, sir. I'm no fan of unfounded rumors. They irk me in particular."

"You probably feel the same way about criminal accusations."

"I do," Isaac agrees. "They irk me as well."

Harold bobs his head and pauses before offering, "Lately I've been wondering if I made a mistake about that welcome sign. You got an opinion on that?"

Isaac shrugs again. "I know it wasn't me, if that's what you're asking."

"Want to tell me what you know?"

"I did already. Except maybe for one thing, which is that for a while I thought Virgil Spintz did it. But now I know he didn't. At least I'm pretty sure of that."

"No, it wouldn't have been Virgil," Harold allows. "I more or less know where he was when the sign was painted."

Isaac has nothing to add to that, and neither does Harold, and after a moment of silence I ask, "Excuse me, Mr. Fassel, but what made you suspect Isaac?"

Harold is obviously humored by my question. "Well, Cecil, Isaac was out that night, and he's a painter. Plus the fact that everyone knows he has a peculiar sense of humor."

Isaac grins. "Thanks for the compliment."

Harold shifts to a serious mode and says, "In light of new evidence that has come to my attention, Isaac, I've decided to speak with Judge Steele and have your summons rescinded . . . if that suits you?"

"Suits me perfectly," Isaac says with alacrity.

"All right, then—unless you hear differently from me, you won't have to appear in court on August fourth. I'll call your father and tell him so."

"Thank you," Isaac says sincerely. "I appreciate that."

Harold studies Isaac and me for a lingering second or so, then tips his hat and turns to depart.

As Deputy Fassel passes through the gate and starts toward his car, I rise from the steps and holler to him, "Just curious—what new evidence have you found?"

Harold turns and gives me a blank look, then smiles. "That information is confidential, Cecil. By the way, you're almost a grown man. You should wear a shirt in public."

"This isn't public. I'm at home."

Harold grunts, gets into his car, and drives away.

Let It Go

The thermometer hits a hundred by three o'clock on Thursday afternoon and stays there until five. Later that evening the temperature drops to eighty-six, but by then I'm too exhausted to enjoy the fourteen-degree easement. I'm afraid I'll spring a leak if I drink any more water.

Mom knows that if she is going to get any sleep, it will be in her air-conditioned office, and she kindly lends me the big fan from her bedroom before retiring for the night. I stick the fan in my window and turn it on full. At ten o'clock I lie atop my bed and start wishing for sleep. It comes only after I've rolled fitfully from side to stomach to side to back for more than an hour . . . and after all that what comes is a dank, sticky sleep less restful than running uphill.

The next morning I awake in an oven. The window fan blows the hot breath of a dragon across my chest. The fan doesn't sound very happy, so I get up and shut it off.

Mom is making coffee when I lumber into the kitchen. On seeing my weary face, she is struck with guilt and compelled to make amends. "You look terrible, Cecil. Go lie down under the air conditioner in my office. You'll feel better in no time."

"Naw. I don't want to disrupt your work. Besides, I prefer suffering on the porch."

"You won't distract me. No need to be a martyr about it."

"It's okay, Mom. I want to sit outside."

She gives me a concerned look. "Hmm."

Friday promises to be even hotter than its predecessor. It's ten-thirty when I step onto the porch and check the thermometer: the mercury flirts with ninety-five. Agh. The prospect of another scorcher would depress me completely if not for a pewter-colored sky. Maybe, just maybe, if everyone in the county behaves, we might just get a thunderstorm later in the day.

Martyrs suffer for a cause. I suffer in the heat for the hell of it (pun intended) and because I have nothing else to do. If pressed, I could probably think of ways to occupy my time, if it wasn't so hot and I wasn't feeling so lazy. But you can't fight reality, and I don't try. I'm sure something will motivate me eventually.

Indeed, just before noon a notion pops into my head and lifts me to my feet. The notion is shaped vaguely like this: On Wednesday night Ariel and I reached a new dimension in our relationship. As she herself put it, "We are closer now." So, I ask myself, Why don't I call her and offer to help decorate for her party? She might be delighted to hear from me. She might suggest I bring a bathing suit and jump in her pool.

I have always admired fine notions and am only rarely able to resist them.

Ariel answers on the second ring. Maybe I'm being paranoid, but she doesn't sound delighted to hear my voice. "Oh, hi, Cecil. What's up?"

"I was just calling to see if you needed any help getting ready for your party."

"It's nice of you to offer, but everything that can't wait until tomorrow is done."

"Uh-huh." My visions of frolicking in the Crisps' big pool evaporate like so many beads of sweat drying on the floor. In the same instant I lose all enthusiasm for speaking on the phone. But I can't just hang up. I must say something. "So . . . how are you?"

"Fine. I'm kind of busy, though."

I can take a hint as quickly as anyone. No need to hit me over the head with a hammer. "Oh, well, then, I'll let you go. See you at the party tomorrow night."

"Right, Cecil. See you here."

Bewildered, I hang up the phone and return to my perch on the porch. What could have happened to change Ariel's attitude in such a brief period? Thirty-six hours ago we were on a heart-to-heart wavelength, yet that is evidently no longer true. Is it the heat? Hormones? Another demonstration of her chronic fickleness? Or—and this is a large OR—am I crazy? Did I mis-read the whole experience and delude myself into thinking that I meant something to Ariel?

With the weather on me like a wool coat, I don't have the patience for a convoluted argument with my ego, so I cut to the truth. "No, Cecil, you're not crazy. Crazy is when you can't find the beginning or the end of a thought. You're just confused emotionally. Actually, you're not even that confused. It's more a matter of your hanging on to a frustrated desire and of projecting that desire at a moving target. Let it go. You don't need the anguish."

I'd get mad right now if it wasn't so damn hot. Maybe I'll feel cooler if I don't think any thoughts. Okay. Go. Don't think.

Stop. You're thinking about nothing. There is no escape from thought.

I jump at the sound of Mom's voice. "You hungry?"

"Naw."

"Something to drink?"

"Maybe in a little while."

With her years of experience, Mom has learned to read my moods, and she knows when to leave me alone. "I'm going to fix tuna fish sandwiches. If you decide you're hungry, there'll be one waiting in the refrigerator for you."

"Thanks. I think I'm going for a walk."

"Suit yourself, son."

The heat has halted all commerce in Bricksburg. The streets are dead. So, it seems, is the cat I see on the courthouse lawn. It lies by a bush with its legs sticking straight up in the air. On closer inspection I realize the cat is breathing. It can sleep wherever it wants in this heat. All dogs that might chase it are hidden under parked cars or porches or wherever there is shade.

My peregrinations carry me through town and out past the high school. I love the word *peregrinate*. It means "to travel, especially on foot." The great thing about peregrinating is that you can do it without a destination. I'm living proof of that.

The sight of the Frosty Treat looming in the near distance brings a sudden grin to my face. Constructed of cinder block and painted pink with green stripes, it would be hard to imagine an uglier little building. My grin is for Gary Perkins, who scoops ice cream in the building four days a week. I'm not so cynical as to be amused because Gary has a menial job—I'm tickled by the pink-and-green-striped jacket his boss requires him to wear. He abhors that jacket almost as much as he hates the pointed hat that goes with it. Not surprisingly, Gary gets irritated when any of his peers drop by to say hello. Even this future Hollywood star cannot lend dignity to a Frosty Treat uniform. The promise of annoying Gary puts a spring in my step.

As I draw closer to my goal I notice Virgil Spintz's BMW parked in the lot. Then—*whoa*—I halt in my tracks. Virgil is sitting at a picnic table with Ariel Crisp.

Well, she did say she was kind of busy. I just didn't expect her to be busy drinking a milk shake with Virgil.

I turn, tuck my tail between my legs, and start back toward town, hopefully before Ariel or Virgil sees me on the road. I'm not proud of my retreat—it reeks of emotional immaturity—but it sure feels like the right thing to do. At any rate, all is not lost, for I am not alone in my alienation. With Ariel and Virgil just outside his window I can easily imagine that Gary is squirming in his uniform and trying to hide behind the register.

Initially I was stunned by the sight of Ariel and Virgil together, but now, the farther I leave the scene behind, the less it bothers me, until soon I'm actually glad I saw them. People talk about the straw that broke the camel's back; well, in a roundabout manner that's what seeing Ariel just now has done for me. However, I feel the opposite of broken. I feel liberated. In one precise flash of insight my last illusion about Ariel has shattered and a psychological burden has been lifted from my shoulders. As the balladeers sing, "The truth will set you free."

Seeing clearly now, it seems almost funny to think how much effort I put into avoiding and denying the truth in regard to my relationship with Ariel. I might laugh if I didn't feel so pathetic about it. However, I do smile ironically. One vivid insight accompanied by willing acceptance and I have escaped an obsession. I never imagined it would be so simple.

Yet (in my life it seems a *yet* is always waiting in the wings) there is more than one side to the truth. Having broken free of Ariel, what do I find in my mind but an image of Isabel? There she is—her innocent face haunting me like a waking dream. BANG, an anxiety bomb explodes within me. I've been taking Isabel for granted. Have I left her too long? Will she forgive me for ignoring her while I played out a fool's option? Am I a hypocrite for turning to her now, just a guy who woke up suddenly?

I have arrived back on Hickory Street and am within thirty yards of the gate to my yard when I feel a breeze blow over me. At the same time I hear leaves rustling in a nearby tree . . . then the rumble of thunder. Just as I lift my eyes skyward Thor flexes his muscles and a bolt of lightning flashes across the sky. The breeze gives birth to a gust and—one by one—large droplets of moisture splatter upon the sidewalk. Hallelujah. It has begun to rain.

I hear a whoop and turn to see Mr. Henshaw emerging from his house across the street. He prances into the yard and raises his arms to welcome the God-given wetness. After a moment he glances over and catches my eye, but Mr. Henshaw is not embarrassed—he is not going to let some young whipper-snapper cramp his style. And to prove that very point, he starts flailing his raised arms and dancing a little jig. I give him a thumbs-up signal. As Mom once said about Mr. Henshaw, "He is a perfect example of someone marching to the sounds of a different drummer."

I stand where I am for several minutes, letting the rain soak my clothes and hair while I watch Mr. Henshaw dance for joy. At times like this I am inclined to revise my opinion of Bricksburg. So what if the town is a podunk? It's got more than a fair share of original characters.

No Singing in the Lobby

Isabel is waiting in the shade of an oak tree outside her house when Mom and I arrive to pick her up on Saturday morning. She is wearing a dark skirt, a white blouse, stockings, and black buckle shoes. As Isabel starts toward the car Mom says to me in a highly suggestive tone, "Why don't you be a gentleman and give her the front seat?"

I hop out and hold the door open for Isabel. "Good morning. You look nice."

Isabel grimaces. "I look like somebody's secretary."

"Well, then, you sit up front and take notes."

Isabel gives me a cutting look before getting in the car and smiling at Mom. "Hello, Mrs. Rowe," she offers cordially. "Thank you for letting me come along."

"You're more than welcome, Isabel, but I'm the one to be thanking you," Mom says emphatically. "It will be such a pleasure having company while I drive. And do call me Mary."

"I will, Mary."

Say what you wish about southern women, but when it comes to protocol and manners, there is not a more artful social group to be found.

The drive from Bricksburg to Staunton takes two and a half hours. Our route will carry us west through the flat Tidewater region of the state, across the rolling Piedmont plateau, and into the eastern foothills of the Blue Ridge Mountains. In the course of our journey we will drive by hundreds of small farms, over innumerable little creeks and lazy rivers, through dozens of meadows, through hardwood forests and stands of loblolly pine, down long stretches of straight road lined with row after row of corn, past hamlets, villages, and humble towns . . . through the very heart and wounded soul of Civil War country. This is the "Old Dominion." Before we reach our destination, we will drive by countless signs announcing the existence of some historic site or another. They mark shrines to fallen generals and honor fields of bloody battle and give testament to nameless masses lying two feet under in hallowed graves. How many of the signs have ever been vandalized, I'll never know. Presumably they all make legitimate claims.

We are hardly out of King County before Isabel and Mom (whom Isabel now calls Mary) start jabbering like a couple of sisters reunited after a lengthy separation and essentially ignore my presence in the backseat. It's a frustrating situation for me. On several occasions I lean forward and attempt to participate in their conversation, but my comments are welcomed as little more than anecdotal tidbits and not effectively incorporated into the dialogue. Obviously, there's only room for two on the communications wave they are riding.

Fine. Let them talk. I'll brood here in the backseat and save my energy for Aunt Jane. The woman has a unique capacity for exhausting her visitors. Although, as I said earlier in these pages, June's condition is not compounded by paranoiac delusions, she is by no means exempt from pain and suffering. We all struggle emotionally from time to time. With June the conflict is constant and in her case amplified by confusing divisions in her personality. When she attempts to gain perspective on her own feelings, she does so without the benefit of a singular identity. In other words, she doesn't always know which part of herself is feeling what. Consequently it is difficult for her to mentally resolve her conflicts and she is forced to ride them out—forced to wait until they wind down of their own accord. What frequently happens is that June winds down before her conflicts do and she falls asleep, often abruptly, sometimes in midsentence. Although she is not technically a narcoleptic, an untrained observer might surmise that she is.

The miles roll by and the conversation in the front seat does not wane. Finally I see a sign informing us that Staunton, Virginia, is the birthplace of Woodrow Wilson, the twenty-eighth president of the United States of America. We are almost there. Western State Hospital is just a few miles across town.

Founded in 1825, the hospital was originally called Western Lunatic Asylum, but for several reasons (not the least of which was the evolving sensibilities of the public), the name was changed in 1894. The facility consists of more than a dozen large, multistoried brick buildings situated on approximately thirty acres of elevated land on the west side of Staunton. The entire complex is surrounded by an ominous chain-link fence topped with coils of razor wire. Many of the buildings have heavy iron grates on the windows.

Despite its daunting appearance, Western State Hospital has a commendable history of humane and progressive treatment of its patients. For example, in 1906 it was one of the first of its kind to dispense with the use of straitjackets and other forms of mechanical restraints, except in violent cases, and in recent years that practice has been abandoned altogether. Attending doctors now have psychoactive drugs available that are powerful enough to immobilize a rogue elephant.

As Mom turns from the street and we approach the hospital gate I study Isabel's reflection in the rearview mirror. Her apprehension is apparent. She sits tensely forward with her eyes fastened on the buildings in the distance. I'm not surprised by her reaction. I've been visiting the place for seventeen years and I still get slightly spooked when I view the fortresslike fence surrounding the compound.

Mom gives Isabel a concerned look, then catches my eye in the mirror and makes a face that says, "Well, here we go." I nod to say, "I understand, and I agree." All the while Isabel's gaze does not waver from the imposing brick structures on the hill.

Mom slows to stop at the gate, but the guard recognizes her and waves us through without delay. We proceed about an eighth of a mile to the top of the hill, then turn right, continue another thousand yards, and park in front of the Stribling Building. This is where Aunt June lives. It is a vine-covered, dormitory-style building nestled peacefully in a cluster of old trees.

"You'll be fine," Mom says to Isabel in a reassuring tone as we ascend the three steps to the entrance.

I pull the door open and add, "Just pretend it's a movie."

Mom reprimands me with a stern look.

"What?" I shrug defensively. "I was being lighthearted."

Isabel smiles wanly. "Please, don't worry about me."

We enter the lobby and are instantly swallowed up by Louisa Bey's effusive presence. She has risen from her desk and hurried forward to give Mom a hug. Louisa has been the head nurse in the Stribling Building since long before I was born, and although Mom and I sometimes joke that she is a patient parading as a hospital administrator, we don't believe that for a second. What we do believe is that Louisa Bey is one of the most compassionate and competent mental health practitioners in the world. She also happens to be a huge fan of Aunt June. After Louisa disengages from Mom, I shake her hand, and while Mom introduces Louisa to Isabel, I look over at Louisa's desk to see if the No Singing in the Lobby sign is still there. It is.

One day a couple of years ago, after repeatedly seeing and wondering about the sign, I asked Louisa why it was there. She told me a rather amusing story, which I will now pass on to you. I do so because the story is funny, not because I wish or intend to mock the mentally ill. Crazy people do not plan to go crazy. They do not set out purposively to be insane. Much like aging, it's just something that happens to them. And like old people, they deserve all the respect anyone will give them.

One of the long-term patients currently living in the Stribling Building is a short little man with a round face named Leonard Landford. He bounces when he walks and he looks to be about sixty years old. Although I doubt if Leonard has ever traveled outside the state of Virginia, he claims he was once a successful Broadway producer, and he is wont to back up his claim by singing the lyrics he has memorized for any of several dozen show tunes from the 1950s and 1960s. He isn't much of a singer, but he sure is loud, and before Louisa finally put a stop to it, the entrance lobby was Leonard's favorite venue. The way Louisa told the story, every day at noontime, Leonard would appear in the lobby, surrounded by some of the building's less discerning residents, and begin wailing the words to songs from *Hello, Dolly!* or *My Fair Lady* or whatever struck his fancy.

On each occasion Louisa would remind Leonard that singing in the lobby was not allowed, and without fail or offering any argument he would promptly curtail his performance and depart for the recreation hall, where screaming was permitted. The next day he would return at noon and begin to sing anew. This went on for what Louisa claimed seemed like a year, and then she had the idea of making the sign and putting it on her desk. It worked like magic. The next time Leonard appeared with his followers, Louisa pointed to the sign and told him that no singing in the lobby was now an official rule. Leonard looked at the sign, drew a long face, huffed at Louisa, and led his troops away. Since then he hasn't been back to sing, and when his travels do carry him through the lobby, he limits himself to humming softly.

I've said hi to Leonard a couple of times, but he always ignores me. When I asked for June's opinion on the man, she said she thought he was a hard nut to crack. That's a quote.

As Louisa ushers us toward the stairway she hails an orderly and sends him ahead to alert Aunt June to our arrival. Louisa would normally accompany us up to June's room, but today she is short of help.

Galactic Jets

Aunt June has a corner room on the third floor. It's at the far end of the building, opposite from where the stairs meet the hallway. The orderly that Louisa sent up ahead of us is waiting when we reach the third-floor landing. He informs us that June is ready for company, then shuffles off to deal with a television set that someone has cranked up to full volume.

As we start down the long hallway Isabel seems even more tense than she was in the car. Deciding that small talk will do her good, I sidle over and attempt to bolster her confidence with flattery. "You know, it was your joke about the secretary. Not mine. I was serious when I said you looked nice."

Isabel accepts the compliment in stride. "That's kind of you to say so, Cecil . . . whether or not it's true."

I nod insistently. "It's true, all right."

Her eyebrows dart up, then down, and she says, "Thank you."

June's room is L-shaped, with her bed and closet space separated from the living area by a curtain. A window on the west end of the room opens into the upper branches of a massive oak tree. A table and chairs are positioned by the window. Next to them is a sofa pushed against the wall. Across from the sofa is a floor-to-ceiling bookshelf crammed with so many books, magazines, and papers it appears ready to spit out items at any moment. The room is painted pea green, a color that psychologists say has a calming effect on humans. Although June would be provided with a television if she wished, she does not have one in her room. She thinks televisions are evil. She calls them lobotomy boxes.

Mom reaches to knock at June's door, and after a brief pause we hear June shout, "Who is it?"

"It's Mary. I'm with Cecil and a friend."

A substantial pause follows before June replies from the far end of the room, "Come in."

When we enter, June is sitting on the sofa, holding an issue of *Vogue* magazine. She looks up and smiles as if pleasantly surprised by neighbors dropping in on their way home from the store. Casually, June sets her magazine on the floor and rises. She is wearing onyx earrings, a salmon-colored blouse, tan slacks, and brown loafers. As usual, her hair is perfectly arranged.

As Mom moves to hug her sister, Isabel gives me a startled look. I think she is surprised by June's attractiveness, and with good reason, for June does not fit the mental patient stereotype. Indeed, as Mom proclaims when she and June part from their embrace, "You get prettier every time I see you."

June agrees. "Yes, I suppose I do."

I extend a hand and step forward. "Hi, Aunt June. How've you been?"

June looks me over from head to toe before taking my hand and replying, "I've been much the same, Cecil. And you? Have you been keeping out of trouble?"

"Well, I haven't been arrested lately."

"Your luck is holding, then," June chides me with a wink before shifting her attention to Isabel. "Who is that lovely creature behind you?"

I turn and gesture. "This is a friend of mine from Bricksburg. Her name's Isabel. Isabel, meet my aunt June."

"How do you do?"

"That varies tremendously," June notes as she accepts Isabel's proffered hand into hers. "Sometimes I'm up, sometimes I'm down, and sometimes I go sideways. Do you eat many apples?"

Isabel answers with a flustered blush, "I eat a fair amount. I like apples."

"Ha. I knew it," June says with a triumphant little laugh. "I could tell from looking at your complexion. Apples have pectin in them, and you have perfect color."

"Thank you."

"Don't thank me for being envious." June releases Isabel's hand and studies her face with unabashed scrutiny. "If I had skin like yours, I'd throw away all my cleansers, creams, moisturizers, and emollients. Oh, maybe I'd keep a few creams."

Mom, determining that it's time to rescue Isabel, takes June by the arm and turns her toward the sofa. "Let's get comfortable while we talk."

Isabel and I move to sit in the chairs at the table, and as we get settled June aims a rather dubious stare in my direction. She holds it for a second or two, glances quickly at Isabel, then sighs and says to Mom, "I do wish you would have invited me to the wedding, Mary. He is my nephew."

Mom winces slightly. "You weren't invited because there was no wedding."

"Postponed?"

"They're friends, June. They are not engaged."

June affects an incredulous look and blasts me with a disapproving frown. "What's the matter with you, Cecil? Don't you astronauts get paid enough to live on?"

I've never been entirely sure whether June believes I am training to become an astronaut or if she's merely perpetuating a running joke. Whatever. I follow her lead. "They pay all our expenses and we get a small salary."

June huffs at me and says to Isabel, "It's the uniforms that make them arrogant. They take one look at themselves in the mirror and start thinking they're better than normal folks."

"June, June," Mom repeats the name softly.

June's eyes widen as she looks at Mom, then she slumps and lowers her head in admonishment. In some ways she reminds me of a child who wants to behave, yet keeps forgetting the rules. At any rate, she keeps her head lowered for all of five seconds before slipping back into her irrepressible self and saying sharply to me, "With Isabel's lovely dermis, you are a fool for not eloping with her. She'll always look younger than she really is. That may not mean much to you now, but it will one day. I can guarantee you that."

I glance at Isabel. She blushes a little, yet does not seem

terribly distressed by June's commentary. That's good, because June isn't ready to drop the matter. "Isabel, are you as smart as you are pretty?"

Mom puts a hand on her sister's arm and says, "Please, June, you're embarrassing Isabel."

June makes and holds eye contact with Isabel for an extended second or two, then turns and informs Mom, "That young lady has gumption. She's not the least bit embarrassed."

Mom removes her hand from June's arm and shrugs.

June sighs and turns again to Isabel. "The world is rough on girls. You should insist that Cecil does the honorable thing."

I'm about to put in my two cents' worth when Mom intercedes. She has had enough. *"June."*

June's face freezes as she perceives that her behavior may be out of line. She folds her hands in her lap and gazes sadly and shamefully at the floor. Her pain is evident. Then, before Mom or I can find words to clear the air, Isabel offers, "I used to get embarrassed at anything. I would walk into a crowded room and feel so self-conscious, I'd want to cry. I don't know why, but I'm better now. I must have grown out of it." June lifts her eyes to Isabel, who continues with a playful smile, "And as for Cecil, he's not the only guy with a uniform."

That tickles Mom and she laughs, which lightens June's mood, and she also laughs. So does Isabel. Fine. Let them laugh. I don't mind. Someone has to play the goat.

June grins at Isabel and jumps right back into the swing of things. "He's fun to tease, don't you think? I worry about him, though . . . he's so young to go adventuring across space. If he isn't careful, a black hole could get him . . . and that would be the end of Cecil."

"A black hole?" says Mom. "June, really."

June pauses thoughtfully for a moment, then informs us all in a gravely poignant tone, "I didn't invent black holes. I'm not that vicious. The cosmos invented them. Black holes are cruel forces of nature."

Half in jest, and half to divert June before she gets too worked up, I offer, "Not to worry. The black holes are marked on our charts. Mission control knows all about them."

"Bah. Mission control. What do they know?" June grimaces. "Black holes are hiding out there like monsters in their lairs. They are the eaters of all things. They swallow entire stars for breakfast . . . but before they do, they chew them up into little pieces."

"Okay," Mom says soothingly. "We know they exist."

June studies me closely. "Promise you'll be careful."

"I promise."

Satisfied with my answer, June turns to Isabel and asks, "Do you know you can tell when you are nearing a black hole?"

Isabel shakes her head.

Of course, June knows the answer. "Galactic jets," she says icily, as if giving a name to the devil.

"What exactly are they?"

June is happy now. She has our undivided attention. "Galactic jets are plumes of stolen light . . . great, long beams of energy sucked into black holes from surrounding stars. If you even get near one, Cecil, it's too late to retreat. By then the black hole has you in its clutches and your little spaceship will have as much chance of getting out as a gnat has of escaping a hurricane."

An awkward silence settles over the room for a moment,

then June frightfully announces, "I'm not even sure we're safe sitting here."

Mom and I exchange concerned glances. We both heard and recognized the telltale edge in June's voice. If her thoughts are not quickly redirected, she may soon start to unravel. Or abruptly wind down. Mom springs to her feet and says, "I'm hungry. Anyone interested in going for lunch?"

"I am." I hop up from my chair.

Isabel reads the situation correctly and rises alongside me. Unfortunately June does not budge from the sofa.

"You coming with us?" Mom asks cheerfully.

"No," June says flatly. "But don't let me keep you. Go ahead. I've got some reading to do."

Mom and I exchange defeated looks. We know from experience that June will not be cajoled into changing her mind. I look at Isabel. She seems to understand that June is struggling. Mom sighs and sits back down beside her sister. "You know, on second thought, I'm not very hungry. June, would you like me to read to you?"

June hesitates.

"What?" Mom says softly.

"If you don't mind, Mary, I'd rather hear Cecil read . . . if he's not going to eat right now."

"Naw. I'm not hungry either. I'd love to read. What do you want to hear?"

The question seems to aggravate June. She stares intently at the overstuffed bookshelf and bites her bottom lip. "You choose, Cecil. Anything but *War and Peace*. I've had just about enough of Prince Andrey for one lifetime."

As I move to select a title from the bookshelf Mom scoots

close to June and puts a protective arm around her sister. Isabel stands where she is by her chair, looking into the oak tree by the window. *The Good Soldier,* by Ford Madox Ford, catches my eye and I withdraw it from the shelf. Returning to my seat, I open the book to part one and begin to read. The first sentence is quite powerful. " 'This is the saddest story I have ever heard.' "

I've been reading for about five minutes when I hear Mom whisper, "That's enough, Cecil. Thank you."

Looking up from the page, I see that June is asleep in Mom's arms.

Fathom This

Isabel, Mom, and I bid Louisa a bittersweet good-bye and walk solemnly out of the Stribling Building. It is not easy leaving June behind, as we do.

It's one o'clock when we stop to eat at a fast-food joint near the outskirts of Staunton. By one-fifteen we are back in the car, heading east over the range of small rolling mountains. The tenor of our return trip to Bricksburg is much different from the morning leg of the journey. Where the westward miles were witness to a stream of friendly chatter, the drive home is characterized by glum silence.

These visits with June take their toll on Mom. She is visibly drained as she grips the steering wheel tightly and withdraws behind a wall of private thought. Except for the concentration needed to watch the road, she is hardly present in the car. Her inner mind has carried her elsewhere. Some would say that was her soul.

I don't believe Mom blames herself for June's schizophrenia, yet I do think she spends a lot of time wondering if there was something she could've done to help prevent or somehow alleviate her sister's illness. Intellectually, Mom understands that June's condition is physiological—that chemicals run amok in the brain are the culprits, not emotional traumas—still she persists in questioning her own role in the matter. That seems unfair to me. Why should Mom have to bear the burden of June's distress? Is there a law in life that says when you care for people deeply, you must experience their sorrows? If there is, it's a bad law and I think it ought to be rewritten.

I'm sure Freud would have something to say about the matter if he were here in the car. He isn't, of course, and frankly I'm glad. Judging from his photograph on the jackets of his books, he strikes me as having been the sort of person who cast a stern pallor wherever he went. Just now I'm not in the mood for stern pallors.

Out of respect for Mom, and because she was genuinely touched by June, Isabel also withdraws silently into herself on the ride home. I study her profile as she gazes out the window and wonder what she is thinking. I cannot even begin to guess, yet it is apparent from the focused stillness of her eyes that her thoughts are running deep. The only way I can describe her stillness is to say it is pinpointed and unwavering. While watching her think, I find myself experiencing an unfamiliar emotion. It's an odd-shaped feeling, containing two essentially contrasting impulses. One says, "Cecil, you might be in love." The other one warns, "You're out of control now." I squelch a sudden urge to climb into the front seat and sit next to Isabel. I can't do that. Not with Mom watching.

Agh. So, here I am again, alone in the rear seat of the car for the second time today, left to keep company with my own imagination. I suppose I should get used to that if I'm going to be a writer. I should make friends with my imagination . . . maybe teach it to do tricks. Or better yet, I could do what Jonathan Swift evidently did and instruct it to dance.

You're getting there, Cecil. You're getting there.

We soon gain the crest of the mountains and start down into the lower plains. My thoughts turn to black holes. What a strange phenomenon! Krol Zandinski explains that black holes are formed when a giant star (it must be a huge one, many times larger than our sun) collapses in on itself with such gravitational force that it implodes into the next dimension and disappears. That's right: The whole star disappears. Now, if you're still with me, try to fathom this: In a black hole the laws of physics are completely destroyed and neither space nor time exists. No space? No time? I guess that's what Aunt June was talking about when she said, "They are the eaters of all things."

The mere concept of a black hole makes me feel petty and small. I mean, next to a black hole, what value does a human being have? What could possibly be the purpose of anguishing over personal problems when there is a force out there that eats stars?

Wrestling with such unanswerable questions, I hardly notice the passing of time. Soon, though, I see the Po River Bridge and realize we are about to enter King County. As we do, Mom emerges from her contemplations and thanks Isabel for coming with us.

Isabel blinks as if waking from a dream. "It was great getting to know you, and I'm glad to have met your sister."

Mom smiles and shrugs. "I'm afraid I wasn't very good company on the ride home."

"You were fine, Mary. I didn't say anything either."

"We should get together soon."

"I'd love that."

"Me too. We'll have tea and pick up where we left off this morning."

"Great."

"Helloooo," I call from the backseat, pitching my voice as if shouting from a distance.

Mom allows a little laugh and gives Isabel a conspiratorial wink. "That must be Cecil. I almost forgot that he came with us today."

"He did?" Isabel giggles.

I'm not sure how I feel about the cozy relationship Mom and Isabel are in the act of establishing. I'm pleased for Mom—she needs more friends she can call her own—yet I get the feeling that separate parts of my life are suddenly blending in an alarming manner. What if Mom becomes Isabel's confidante? And vice versa? At a minimum, that is bound to complicate my home life. Oh, well . . . it's just one more thing to worry about.

We arrive at the Yardleys' at a quarter to four. When Isabel gets out of the car, I hop from the backseat and grab her open door. "I guess I'll see you in an hour or so."

"Right, at the party." Isabel sounds anything but excited.

"You're coming, aren't you?"

Isabel pauses just long enough to make me doubt. "Yes. I'm riding with Isaac and Grace. Grace promised Ariel we'd get there right at five."

"Pauley Harrington is picking me up," I say as I slip into the front seat. Isabel steps back from the car and Mom pulls forward. I add out the window, "Don't forget your dancing shoes."

Isabel gives me an ambiguous look that I am not able to read. It may or may not be meaningful. Whatever. I wave and watch Isabel in the side-view mirror as we drive away. Isabel waves. Then Mom toots the horn.

The Yardleys' driveway is about fifty yards long, and well before we reach the end of it Mom looks askance at me and says, "That's a smart girl."

Oh no. I was expecting this, although not so soon. My reply to Mom is offered in the most casual and detached tone I can muster. "Yeah, she's cool. Isabel is fun."

Mom doesn't say anything. She just smirks.

We Come to His P . . .

The answering machine is blinking when Mom and I return to the house. I hit the playback button and listen: "This is Virgil leaving a message for Cecil at noon on Saturday. I guess you've heard the news by now. I was just wondering what you thought. Call me if you get a chance, or if you don't, I'll see you tonight at Ariel's party."

What news? Oh, well, I'll find out soon enough.

Although it seems somewhat absurd to take a shower shortly before going to a pool party, that is what I do. By twenty to five I've shaved, cleaned my ears, and thrown baby powder under my arms and am looking through the hodgepodge collection of rags that constitute my wardrobe. I am typically an understated dresser, but this evening I'm in a saucy mood . . . and ever so slightly conscious of wanting to impress Isabel. So I go with the khaki trousers I bought last fall, yet have never worn in public. (Gary Perkins always wears khakis, and I don't want to seem as if I'm following his lead.) But what the heck. It's a party. With the pants goes my favorite delphinium blue shirt. It's an oxford button-down that almost matches my eyes. A brown belt, tan socks, and rubber-soled loafers complete the outfit. Into my gym bag go my olive green swim trunks, a towel, a comb, breath mints, and a bottle of Old Spice cologne.

I'm ready to roll at quarter past five when Pauley knocks at the door. I'm relieved to see that he is appropriately attired for the party. He has on weathered jeans, a dappled gray pullover, and flip-flops. Pauley's not a bad-looking guy when he makes the effort. I kick open the screen door and greet him with a firm handshake.

He apologizes for his tardiness. "I would've been here ten minutes ago if I hadn't stopped at the gas station to speak with Eddie Gingrich. You knew someone painted the welcome sign again, didn't you?"

So that was Virgil's news. "No. When?"

"Last night, I think, although I didn't know anything about it until just now, when I drove past the courthouse and saw the sign covered with a tarp. That's why I stopped to speak with Eddie."

"Who was it? What did Eddie say?"

"He wasn't a hundred percent sure. Sheriff Moore and Harold Fassel aren't answering questions, but Eddie heard a rumor that Randolph Crisp was in jail."

Randolph Crisp! There's someone I never considered . . . and yet now that I do, he makes a credible suspect. Vandalizing the welcome sign might just appeal to a middle-aged guy trying to rejuvenate his juices. "What did the sign say?"

Pauley shrugs. "I couldn't see because of the tarp. Eddie didn't know either."

It's immediately clear to me that I cannot let the question go unanswered. I almost feel as if it's my duty to know what has been done to the sign. "So, Pauley, you up for peeking under that tarp?"

"I'm game for that."

I turn and start down the hallway. "Just let me fetch my gym bag and say good-bye to Mom. We'll swing by the courthouse on our way to the party."

So as not to be too obvious about our intentions, we park Pauley's pickup beside the hardware store and pretend to amble idly through town. The precaution is unnecessary. No one pays us the least bit of mind as we approach the courthouse lawn.

The blue plastic tarp that covers the sign is held in place by four bungee cords. Pauley and I—both anxious to do the deed and go—hurriedly unhook the bottom cords and lift the tarp.

At first glance the altered text is difficult to interpret. The freshly applied paint, a green that matches the background, was evidently covered before it could dry properly and has been smeared under the tarp. Even so, you can make out which letters the paint was intended to hide. The *l* in *Welcome* is gone, the *toric* in *Historic* has been painted over, and all of *Bricksburg* has been obliterated except for the letter *B*, which has been altered to make a *P*. I am still trying to make sense of the sign when Pauley reads aloud, "We come to his P—"

"That's what it looks like to me."

"What does *P* mean?"

"Maybe Randolph never finished the job . . . if it was him to begin with. Whoever hit the sign last time used white paint to make new letters."

"You think they caught him in the act?"

"It's possible," I allow as I bend to hook the tarp back in place. "And speaking of caught in the act, let's get out of here before someone sees us."

We return to the pickup and drive north from town toward the Crisps' ten-thousand-square-foot mansion. While Pauley ponders the letter *P*, I worry about whether the party has been canceled. If Randolph is in jail, I doubt Ariel's mother is in any mood for forty rambunctious teenagers running around the house. Indeed, if her husband has been arrested, I imagine Claudia is pitching a hysterical fit right about now.

"*P*? Paaah. Peee. Pooo."

"Don't strain yourself, Pauley. Knowing Mr. Crisp, it could mean anything."

The Crisps' huge brick colonial-style home dominates a low ridge about sixty yards off the highway. I don't know how many acres go with the property, but their nearest neighbors are more than half a mile away on each side of the road. The front yard is manicured to perfection and dotted with ornamental bushes. The pool is behind the house. It is surrounded by a sprawling patio bordered by strips of lawn that are, in turn, surrounded by eight-foot-high privet hedges. (Privets are unusual in King County. This far south, most of the fancy places have box-woods.) Beyond the hedges is an open field with plenty of room for parking.

As Pauley turns at the Crisps' long driveway I see a Clapp

Catering van parked near a side door of the house and take it as an encouraging sign. We proceed past the van and house, then I see numerous familiar cars in the field and know the party is still on.

We pull into the field and park beside Doreen Taylor's canary yellow station wagon. I wave to Marsha Day and Jimmy Lincoln as they get out of Marsha's blue sedan, which is parked next to Virgil's BMW. Marsha and Jimmy are King County's highest-profile and most popular interracial couple. They are a striking pair. Marsha is short and blond, with an extremely fair, almost pink complexion. Jimmy is gangly, tall, and walnut colored.

Pauley hops from the truck and walks about ten yards toward the hedges before stopping to wait for me. I grab my gym bag and give myself a quick inspection in the rearview mirror. Damn this hair. It was fine when I left the house. Oh, well, maybe a dip in the pool will teach it a lesson.

When I catch up to Pauley, he gives me an ill-at-ease look and says, "I've never been to Ariel's house before."

I can appreciate how he feels. The Crisp property is a bit much for a couple of small-town characters like us. Still, it's only real estate. "Relax." I give Pauley a bracing slap on the back. "Adjusting up isn't very difficult. It's stepping down that's hard."

Pauley smiles nervously. "Yeah, right. So, do I look okay? I've got on jeans and you're wearing slacks."

"You look hip," I assure him with a nod. "Wearing flip-flops was a cool idea."

"I've got shoes for later . . . in case I dance, you know."

"That's smart," I tell him, starting toward the gate in the hedges between us and the pool. In the back of my mind I'm hoping that Pauley doesn't try to ride my elbow all night. If that's what happens, I won't be rude to him or anything, but . . . well . . . I am anticipating some private time with Isabel.

Suddenly Pauley exclaims, "Hey, look."

As he speaks I've already begun to read a poster-board sign hanging on the gate. Someone has written in bright red script: *We Come to His Party.*

"There's your *P* for you, Pauley."

Pauley shakes his head and mutters, "Damn. Now who would have thought of that?"

"Only in Bricksburg," I note philosophically.

We swing open the gate and the first person we see—directly ahead of us, bouncing up and down on the diving board—is the man of the hour, Randolph Crisp. So much for being in jail. Randolph is a tall, broad-shouldered man with thick, russet-colored hair, a big Roman nose, and deep-set, gray-blue eyes. Although his stomach may not be as flat as it once was, he's in excellent shape for an older guy, and he obviously isn't shy about showing off his body. He's wearing one of those stretch-tight, European-style swimsuits that emphasize rather than conceal a man's natural bulges. The suit is purple. As Pauley and I enter the pool area and close the gate behind us Randolph bounces a final bounce, springs upward, touches his hands to his toes in a jackknife, and enters the water. His form is not quite so smooth as Isabel's, but it's not bad.

"Hey, Cecil. Pauley. About time you got here."

"Isaac."

"How ya doing?"

"Fine," I say quickly, nodding toward the pool. "So what's the scoop with Mr. Crisp? We heard a rumor he'd been busted for painting the welcome sign."

Isaac nods. "He was. Harold Fassel caught him last night on the courthouse lawn with a can of paint in one hand and a brush in the other. It was him last time too. He proudly admits it."

"And Harold let him walk?"

"No, he spent the night in jail. Mrs. Crisp bailed him out about an hour ago." Isaac turns and grins as we watch Randolph hoist himself from the pool. "You guys just missed it. A few minutes ago Mr. and Mrs. Crisp stood out on the back porch, locking lips in front of everybody. As soon as they were done kissing, Mr. Crisp marched down to the diving board, and that's when you came in."

"Ah man. I would've loved to see that. Anyway, I'm glad they made up."

"So am I. It was a pretty good start for a party. How was your aunt?"

"Okay. Still kooky."

"Isabel said she liked her."

"She liked Isabel too."

This whole time Pauley has been looking around and listening patiently while Isaac and I talk. But now he is ready to join the fun, and he abruptly interjects, "Excuse me, guys. Where can I change into my suit?"

I point to the cabana on our left. "In there. Girls change in the house."

"Thanks," says Pauley, departing immediately for the cabana. I watch him stop en route to speak with Doreen Taylor and Itsy

Nelson. When they both greet him brightly, it occurs to me that Pauley will have no trouble getting into the swing of things.

"Come on," says Isaac, turning and motioning for me to follow. "Let's go snitch some hors d'oeuvres in the kitchen. Grace and Isabel are in there, watching Ariel and Mrs. Crisp boss around the caterers."

At the sound of Isabel's name I feel a little jump in my chest. It's a new jump for me. I like it.

Taking a Dive

Isaac and I are crossing the rear deck on our way to the kitchen when we encounter Isabel, in her swimsuit, coming out the door. He continues into the house. I stop to speak with his little sister. As our eyes meet I feel strangely self-conscious. It's the first time I can remember her doing that to me. Nothing has actually happened between us, yet in my mind, everything has changed. She senses it too. Or maybe she is just reflecting back my nervous energy. "I was hoping I'd find you."

"And you did."

"How are you?"

My question appears to amuse Isabel. "Well, Cecil, I'm fine. How are you?"

"Can't complain. I'm ready for a party."

Her amusement grows. "You came to the right place, then. I'm ready for a dip."

"I can see that. So . . . I guess I'll catch up with you later."

She arches an eyebrow and gives me a pointed look. "You better."

"I will," I mumble as she departs for the pool. I'm not sure, but I think she was being flirtatious.

More and more guests continue to arrive at the party and I get distracted wandering around, saying hello to different people. It's after six before I make my way to the cabana and change into my bathing suit. Then, when I emerge into the pool area, Randolph Crisp says my name and approaches with his right hand extended.

"Hello, Mr. Crisp." I shake his hand.

"Drop the mister, will you? It makes me feel old."

"Yes, sir, Randolph."

"Say, how's your mother's book coming?"

"Slowly but surely," I reply, surprised he knows she is writing a book.

Mr. Crisp nods and rubs his chin thoughtfully. "I suspect she's onto something. Not only are there too many people on the planet, but most of them don't know why they're here. That's a quote, Cecil. You can tell Mary I said that."

"I'll pass it on. Maybe when the book comes out, I'll be able to get you a complimentary copy."

"Nonsense. I'll buy one off the shelf."

There's nothing to say to that, so I just nod. A part of me wants to ask Randolph what inspired him to paint the welcome sign, but I'm not a complete social goof. I suppress my curiosity and offer small talk instead. "Good crowd, huh?"

Mr. Crisp seems confused by my comment. He gives me an odd look, hesitates, then says with a shrug, "Excuse me while I go flirt with my wife. I'm a bit behind on my attentions there."

"Sure. Go ahead," I reply. "Don't let me keep you."

A sudden grin breaks out on Mr. Crisp's face. "You're a good egg, Cecil. Nothing wrong with you that a professional haircut wouldn't fix."

I watch with keen interest as the man strides across the patio area to the deck on the back of the house, where Claudia Crisp is waiting. He bounds up the steps, engulfs her in his arms, and kisses her smack on the lips. (If that's called flirting, I've got a few things to learn.) Somehow, although we chatted for only five minutes or so, I'm left with the fond impression that I know and understand Randolph Crisp. He seemed sane enough to me. If he does have a behavioral problem, I suspect it has more to do with testosterone than psychology. His remark about my hair reminds me that it's time to get in the pool.

I see Isabel waiting in line at the diving board and go to stand behind her. "Having fun?"

She answers with a pert smile, and in a flash I realize without a doubt that she is the girl for me. Of course, I'll need to confirm that with her, which is what I am just about to do when the board clears for Isabel. "Watch this," she says.

"I'm watching," I reply, expecting a variation of the swan dive she often executes from Billy Goat Bridge.

She squares herself on the board. Her arms drop to her sides; she draws a breath, takes three quick steps, bounces upward, tucks, grabs her ankles, and spins. It's a flip. Her release is timed perfectly.

As Isabel rises to the surface and shakes water from her thick black hair the poolside crowd erupts in a spontaneous outpouring of applause. The audience's exuberance inspires me as much as Isabel's daring, and on a whim I decide to make my first dive of the day a forward one-and-a-half. I walk purposefully to the end of the board and test its resiliency, then turn, measure my stride backward, and pause to visualize my movements. A murmur of anticipation passes around the pool. I tell myself, *Go.* Half step, full step, high step, and jump. I have the height. I have the spin . . . yet not quite enough of either. Whap! I slap the surface with my chest and face. I can't even tell you how much that *stings*.

The crowd is less than forgiving. "BELLY FLOP."

"Cecil eats it!"

"Let's see that again."

After my vision clears, my ears stop ringing, and my sense of direction returns, I swim to the side of the pool and try to pretend nothing unusual has occurred. However, the peanut gallery knows differently. "No, I don't need an ambulance," I answer one question. "My privates are fine," I reply to the next. "No, I haven't been practicing."

At this juncture I am saved from further humiliation as Itsy Nelson walks tentatively to the end of the board, where she stops and looks down. It is a mere three feet to the surface, yet Itsy is obviously reluctant to make the plunge. Seconds pass, and her reluctance grows into terror. Doreen and Pauley move to either side of the board and offer encouragement. "Just jump," Doreen urges. "Water is soft. It won't hurt you."

"You can't do worse than Cecil," says Pauley. "And look at him. He's still alive."

I shoot a stern look in Pauley's direction, but he knows that I know he is just joking, and he laughs.

With everyone now watching Itsy, I pull myself from the pool and grab a towel off a nearby table. Isabel approaches and gives me a sympathetic look, yet does not utter a word about my dive. The world would be a lot nicer place to live if more people were as tactful as Isabel.

Meanwhile Itsy stands frozen on the end of the board.

Ariel is sitting on a chaise longue across the pool from where Isabel and I are standing. She's wearing a little sun hat and clad in a gold-colored bikini that strains the limits of modesty in King County. (Ariel would stick out in France.) She is flanked by Virgil Spintz on her right and Gary Perkins on her left, with Watson McGee hovering in the general vicinity. Slowly she turns her gaze from Itsy to me and calls loudly, "We have aloe vera in the house. Want me to get it for you?"

I shake my head. "I'm fine."

Gary is unable to resist taking a dig. "No question about your dive, Cecil, it was the best one-and-a-quarter I've seen so far this year."

I just sneer at Gary, and I'm pleased to see Virgil doing the same. If possible, Virgil has less tolerance for Gary Perkins than I do. After a moment Virgil turns and hollers for all to hear, "I guess you got my message. We'll talk later, okay, Cecil?"

"Sure," I shout. "I would've called you back, but I was in Staunton all day."

"I heard. So, things panned out all right, didn't they?"

"Yep." I smile knowingly, hopefully mysteriously, aware that several people have taken note of the friendly tone between Virgil and me. I suppose, in a manner of speaking, we have just made our public debut as pals.

Not to be left out for long, Ariel sits up in her chair, catches

Isabel's eye, and calls with affected concern, "It might soothe Cecil's chest if you rubbed baby oil on him. There's a bottle on the table behind you."

Isabel tenses ever so slightly and levels a steady stare at Ariel. A glint in her eyes declares that she will not be mocked.

Ariel is unprepared for Isabel's defiance, and for a moment she seems flustered. Finally, when she finds her voice and speaks again, her tone is conciliatory. "It was just a thought, Isabel. You probably don't want to get your hands all oily."

Isabel's lips turn up in a hint of a smile. "Not now."

Ariel eyes Isabel with what appears to be newfound respect, then flashes a smile of truce and returns her gaze to Itsy. Poor thing. She's still stuck on the end of the board.

I incline my head to Isabel. "Good work."

Isabel huffs. "Ariel Crisp should know better than to get catty with me."

That makes me chuckle. "You're cute when you get mad."

"Cute?"

I backtrack fast. "You know, pretty."

Isabel softens a little, but not completely. "I'm going to change before the barbecue starts. If you want, meet me on the middle patio in a few minutes."

"I'll be there," I agree, then add, "By the way, Isabel, you're pretty anyway, even when you aren't mad."

Isabel presses her lips into a frown that contains the smallest hint of a smile. "I didn't say anything earlier about your dive, Cecil, but it's clear to me now that it rattled your senses."

"My senses are intact," I counter. "Can't you handle a little flattery?"

As Isabel pauses to consider my question, there is an almost wounded look in her eyes that suggests her feelings have been hurt. That look fills me with regret and I am on the verge of apologizing for my insensitivity when she informs me, "Flattery is fine if you mean it, Cecil."

I don't even think about my reply; the words volunteer themselves. "I do, Isabel. I think you are beautiful."

Finally an unambiguous smile appears on Isabel's face. This is my reward for being honest. It's getting hard to see well in the diminishing twilight, but I think I can see a touch of pink in her cheeks. "Meet me on the patio," she says before hurrying into the house to change.

I linger where I am for another five minutes and watch the Itsy Nelson drama. I should say, comedy. It ends only after Pauley leaps onto the board and threatens to manhandle her into the pool. In her attempt to get away from Pauley, Itsy accidentally steps off the board and falls thirty-six inches into the water below. She starts thrashing even before her head goes under, which it barely does. In the next instant she realizes she is safe and triumphantly raises a fist. The crowd bursts into a chorus of wild cheers.

As I drink in the mirthful sounds and observe the many happy faces around me I am nearly overwhelmed with contentment. This is my planet. I am Cecil from Bricksburg. These are my friends. This is my life.

Scent of the High Seas

After dressing in my party attire, combing my hair into submission, and slapping Old Spice on my chest and cheeks, I exit the cabana with my head held high, excited about my scheduled rendezvous with Isabel. The caterers have lit the charcoal grills they brought with them and set up on a patch of grass between the pool and the privets. Next to the grills are two cloth-covered tables. One of the tables holds platters of uncooked hamburger, hot dogs, and marinated chicken parts, as well as bowls of macaroni and potato salad. Beverages are being served at the second table. I grab a soda for myself and an ice tea for Isabel.

Although this is supposed to be an alcohol-free party, a few indulgent characters have been sneaking off to their cars to indulge in nips of the hard stuff. It's the usual group (Danny Albright, Jake Coburn, Shelly Mills, and Ricky Talley), and they now jostle together near the shallow end of the pool, making lewd comments and laughing loudly at their own dulled senses. They presume to entertain everyone within hearing distance, when in fact they amuse only themselves.

I claim an unoccupied table in a corner of the patio and sit facing the pool. The table and chairs around it, like the cabana and every piece of outdoor furniture in sight, are festooned with colorful ribbons and paper streamers. These decorations are the handiwork of Ariel and Grace, and I must say, they add a certain festive element to the scene.

It isn't long before Isabel appears on the back deck and starts down the steps toward the patio area. She's wearing a short jean skirt, a sleeveless white blouse, and baby blue sneakers. Her wet black hair is combed straight back over her shoulders. As she draws closer into the light I make a mental note that she isn't wearing makeup. That isn't unusual—she never wears makeup—yet now that Aunt June has drawn my attention to Isabel's complexion, I have a heightened appreciation for her natural blush. June seemed to think the eating of apples was a factor. To me it appears as though Isabel has been eating roses. But what do I know? Not much, evidently, for when she smiles and sits down at the table beside me I suddenly avow, "Isabel, I've been a fool."

Such statements invite witty retorts, and Isabel gives me the one I no doubt deserve. "I've always thought that might be the case, Cecil, but what prompts you to say so now?"

"You," I answer, leaning forward to explain. "I've been looking at you for years, but I only recently realized what I was seeing. Who, I mean. Not what."

Isabel studies me with a patient smile. She realizes I am trying to say something important. "If you don't mind, perhaps you could elaborate."

"Perhaps," I allow with a shrug, and sit back. "But to be honest, it's all just coming to me now. I haven't really had time to organize my thoughts."

The impulse of a reply rises to Isabel's lips, but she does not give it voice. She wants me to continue.

I pause, and in the back of my mind I think of what Isaac said about life being short, and that if you weren't making the best of it you should at least be making the most of it. That's a simplistic base for a philosophy, yet it seems reasonable to me and I decide to adopt it. Here goes nothing. "Okay . . . Isabel, you know how in Russian novels and lots of Hollywood movies there's this thing called 'love at first sight.' "

Isabel nods. She does.

"Well . . . what I'm thinking of is the opposite. Not completely opposite, but you know what I mean. I hope you do. I, ah . . . don't know how else to say it."

Isabel sees that I'm sinking and buoys me up with a bright smile. "You're good with words, Cecil. I'm sure you could find another way to express yourself if you really tried. But I hear you. I catch your drift."

I look straight into the lucid pools of Isabel's eyes, and what I see confirms that she does understand . . . and she approves. I sit forward again. "Before I continue and embarrass myself forever, I want to say that you were really sweet today with Aunt June. And I'm sure you know you've got my mom wrapped around your little finger."

"Both your mom and your aunt are wonderful people," Isabel

replies, but she's not interested in talking about them right now. "Go on with what you were saying, Cecil. I liked what I was hearing."

"You did?"

"Don't you know that?"

The sincere and simple manner of Isabel's response tells me all that I want to know, and more. I am suddenly freed of doubt and no longer struggle with my self. This is great. I guess when two people are romantically suited for each other, things are supposed to go smoothly. I draw a breath and offer, "Okay, here's what I think I feel. It's clear to me—"

"There they are!"

"We thought you two had left."

"Hi, Grace. Hi, Isaac."

"We aren't interrupting anything, are we?" Grace grins. She knows perfectly well that she and Isaac have caught the two of us in an intimate moment.

"Nothing important," Isabel answers in a mildly sarcastic tone. "Cecil was about to reveal the number of his secret Swiss bank account. That's all."

Isaac gives me an innocent look and shakes his head. I think he's trying to inform me that Grace made him come with her to our table. When he plops down in one of the unoccupied chairs, I tell him, "Make yourself comfortable."

Grace giggles. "We'll go elsewhere if you want."

"Don't leave now." The tone of my sarcasm is more saucy than Isabel's. "Please," I plead, slumping down in my seat. "I beg you to stay."

Isabel gestures toward the remaining chair. "Sit, Grace. If you don't, someone else will."

Grace settles herself in the remaining chair, moans happily, and looks around at her three companions. There is something quirky and humorous about Grace's expression, and none of us are able to keep from smiling, however subtly. That's all the encouragement that Grace needs. She claps and squeals. I won't try to make the scene clearer than that; it's one of those little moments that happen between friends.

As Grace slowly gains control of herself and begins to breathe regularly again, Isaac wriggles his nose and sniffs at the air. "Hmm. I believe I can smell the high seas. Someone at this table must be wearing Old Spice."

"Yes . . . and it is such a sensuous aroma," says Grace, her nostrils flaring.

Isabel throws back her head and laughs. "A truly masculine scent."

I slump even farther down in my chair. Try though I do, I cannot think of a witty retort. Oh, well. One will come to me later.

After a few minutes we all rise and move to the rear of the line that has suddenly formed beside the food table. I see Pauley up ahead of us, sandwiched between Doreen and Itsy. I say his name and salute. When Pauley waves and grins hello, it occurs to me that I've never seen him happier. Nor Itsy, for that matter. The two of them seem to have found a harmonious groove. Soon Isabel whispers in my ear, "Look smart. Here comes our hostess."

Ariel has changed from her bikini into white slacks, an apricot-colored blouse, and tan pumps with ankle straps. She works the line like a professional canvasser, greeting each of her guests one by one, flashing her camera-ready smile at all. When she comes to Pauley, she really turns on the charm. I don't know if she knows I'm watching and is being extra nice to him for my benefit. It doesn't matter. I am pleased for Pauley's sake. He deserves all the social points he can score. "I'm so glad you could make it, Pauley," Ariel gushes warmly. "I wasn't sure if Cecil got you the message or not."

Pauley spills over with gratitude. "I got it, and thanks a million for inviting me. This is a great party. I'm having a blast."

Ariel assumes a modest air. "That's all I ask for. I hope everyone feels that way."

"Don't know why they wouldn't," Pauley declares.

Ariel gives Itsy a playful wink. "Make sure he doesn't have too much fun."

Itsy giggles mischievously. "I'll watch him."

Ariel moves to Grace and puts an arm around her waist. They buss cheeks. Ariel smiles hello to Isaac and me, nods politely to Isabel, and asks our little group, "What's happening here with the in crowd? Everything up to your measure?"

"Absolutely."

"Perfect setup for a party."

"Love those decorations."

"We're so lucky to be your friends."

Ariel soaks up the praise, then turns to Isabel and makes an obvious and seemingly sincere effort to establish peace between them. "We never hang out. We should change that in the future."

"We should." Isabel accepts the olive branch. "I have to tell you, that's a beautiful blouse. I love apricot."

Ariel puckers her lips and leans forward. I think for a second that she intends to kiss Isabel, but then Isabel smiles approvingly and says, "Cool. Matching lipstick."

"Tastes like apricots too," Ariel adds, then asks, "Did Cecil tell you about our heart-to-heart the other night?"

Isabel glances in my direction. "He never mentioned it."

Before I can begin to explain, Ariel replies, "I'm sure that's because I asked him to keep it private. Cecil is very good when he gives his word. I wish more people were dependable like him."

Blushing, I volunteer to Isabel, "We were talking about her dad."

"If it wasn't for Cecil, I would have had a nervous breakdown." Although Ariel has wildly exaggerated my influence, I appreciate her support. Our eyes meet for a second and a shared understanding passes between us. She knows I have let go of my desire for her, and she knows I know she knows. (Pardon the alliteration.) A veil seems to lift from in front of me, and in a flash of insight I realize that Ariel values my friendship. She truly wishes me well and I feel the same for her.

A commotion at the gate draws Ariel's attention and she says, "Well, well. It's the Land Sharks. I've been wondering when they'd decide to get here."

No one in our group says anything as we watch Ariel sashay off to meet the band. We all know she's one of a kind. The line moves forward, and soon it is our turn to fill our plates with food.

I'm with Her

There is a scientific maxim that says opposites attract. It may hold true with elemental compounds, but I don't believe it is applicable to people. Humans are far more complex than organic substances, and never are they exactly the opposite of each other. With humans the line is blurred. Humans have too many varied dimensions. Just consider how each of us builds up and creates our own personality. We do so step by step, like travelers on a long journey collecting postcard experiences that are then filed in individualized compartments called brains. First we file the experiences, then later, usually on whim, we call them up and analyze them through the lenses of our own, unique prejudices. People are not electric charges separated into pluses and minuses. We are evolving entities experiencing life in a strange, vast, and ever expanding universe. There is no scientific maxim to tell us why we are attracted to whom and when. The mystery of romance, like the enigmatic essence of nature itself, cannot be codified into a predictable formula. It is what it is, and that's the way it should be.

Isabel and I stand at the edge of the patio, listening to the amplified sounds of the Land Sharks, watching a dozen or so fun-loving people contort and shake their bodies in rhythmic time to the music. She leans to speak in my ear. "Excellent dance band, don't you think?"

I nod in agreement and shout, "None of that experimental rock from the Land Sharks."

"Wow," Isabel exclaims, and points. "Get a load of Mr. and Mrs. Crisp. They're really getting down."

I watch as the happily reunited pair gyrate their hips, bounce from foot to foot, and roll their heads from side to side. "Yeah, they've got it going. So . . . Isabel, I never finished what I was trying to say earlier."

"I know. You hardly got started."

"Want to go somewhere and talk?"

"Later. Look at Pauley go."

"Right."

"What's with your sour tone?"

"Nothing."

"Then quit frowning."

I try to obey, but at best, my frown becomes a pout.

Isabel reaches to take my hand. "What's the matter, Cecil?"

I hem and haw, then try to explain. "I guess I'm a little disappointed, that's all. I thought you wanted to hear what I had to say."

Isabel heaves such a loud sigh, I can hear it over the music. "Cecil, I'm interested in everything you want to say. But later. Right now I want to dance."

That hurts, yet at the same time I'm persuaded. "Then let's dance," I agree, turning and starting for the center of the patio. Isabel doesn't budge, and since we're still holding hands, I am brought up short. When I turn, she gives me a meaningful look. Somehow I know what to do. We meet halfway, our lips parted for kissing.

Our kiss is more tender than heated. I've never felt anything more natural in all of my life. After several long, magical seconds Isabel breaks away. Yet I'm not ready to stop kissing. I pull her back to me and our lips meet once again. It never crosses my mind to wonder if anyone is watching. I don't care.

We must have stopped kissing at one point. I don't remember when. The next thing I do recall is us in the middle of the crowd . . . bobbing, dipping, and shimmying to the hard-driving sounds of the Land Sharks.

I find it curious to note: Although there are over forty people at the party, most of them my friends, for the next two hours I am exclusively aware of Isabel Yardley . . . and of myself, whom I cannot help but notice because I'm with her.

I'm with her. I like the sound of that.

November Addendum

More than three months have passed since Isabel and I connected as a couple at Ariel's party. In the larger scheme of things, three months is hardly a blink of the cosmic eye. For example, light emanating from Alpha Centauri (the nearest star to our sun) on that night in early August has traveled a mere one and a half trillion miles and still has twenty-four trillion miles to go before reaching earth four years from now. And yet in the smaller scheme of human existence, a substantial amount of living can be accomplished in a three-month period. (Contrary to Einstein's radical claim, time is not an illusion.) Plenty of personal changes can be made in ninety days and nights, and that is what has happened in Bricksburg. The town hasn't changed—it remains the same funky podunk it always was—yet several of its citizens are no longer who they once were.

One change of paramount importance to me: Today, Saturday, November seventh, at approximately eleven o'clock, I obtained my Virginia State driver's license. The test went off without a hitch. I simply ignored the little skirt Faye was wearing and kept my eyes on the road.

So far, except for driving home after the test, I haven't gone anywhere with the car. Mom took it this morning but said she'll be back this afternoon and promised I could use it when she returns. I can hardly wait to hold those keys in my hand. Isabel and I have plans to hit the road. We're not sure where we're going, other than we know it will be in the countryside. That way when night comes, we can lie side by side on the ground and study the stars. We've been doing a lot of that lately.

I've been learning a lot from Isabel. She's been teaching me that it's possible for people to change for the better. It isn't easy to do so, yet if they try hard enough, they can alter and improve their approach to life and thereby become better people. When this happens, it's a boon for everyone, for as Isabel says, improved characters make for improved societies. According to her, it is our duty as social beings to accept and support anyone we know who is trying to make positive changes.

I admire the concept, and with Isabel's caring support, I've recently been experimenting with changing a few of my own attitudes. So as not to overwhelm myself, I've limited my initial experiment to two attitudes in particular. They are listed below.

Attitude experiment one: I've recently been keeping a tight rein on my tendency to think that most people are crazy. I see now that it was a cynical, arrogant habit . . . a lazy way to cope with feelings that were hard to understand. Just because someone doesn't view the universe the way I do, it doesn't necessarily follow that the person is nuts. Each to His (or Her) Own is my new motto.

Attitude experiment two: I have opened my mind to the possibility that Gary Perkins is a likable person. Surprisingly, this adjustment has not been as challenging as I presumed it would be. A few weeks ago, Isabel, Grace, Ariel, Virgil, Isaac, and I drove over to the Binkerton town hall to see Gary perform in a stage adaptation of *Candide*, by Voltaire. (Voltaire, like Swift, wrote satire. Voltaire's work is a little more hard hitting than Swift's, and almost as funny.) Gary acted the part of Doctor Pangloss, who was a determined optimist in a problem-filled world. I must admit, Gary played the part convincingly, and in my view, he stole the show. Who knows? Maybe his dream of making it in Hollywood isn't so far-fetched after all. Anyhow, now that I've seen him do what he does best, it's much easier to perceive him as likable. I wish him luck.

Speaking of luck, perhaps Gary should go shake hands with Randolph Crisp. Although the man was caught on the courthouse lawn with a can of paint in one hand and a brush in the other, and although he confessed to previously desecrating the welcome sign, no criminal charges were filed against him. He wasn't even fined. Of course, Randolph had more than luck on his side: He had charitable power, spelled *money*, and with it he offered to pay for the new wing the Bricksburg Volunteer Rescue Squad has been wanting for the past five years. Clearly Randolph's generosity had a lot to do with Judge Steele's decision to look the other way. Still, you have to give Mr. Crisp credit for turning a bad situation into a good one. Nowadays when his name comes up in public, instead of being criticized as a social pariah, he is hailed as a civic hero. Actually, Randolph is not always hailed when his name gets mentioned. I hear

Trudy Benson is still hopping mad about the way he dropped her and went home to his wife.

Soon after the big party, Mr. and Mrs. Crisp began driving to Richmond once a week to see a marriage counselor. It must be working because they both seem happy every time I see them. Ariel has a different take on the matter. She says the counselor is a waste of money and that what is really helping her parents are the restaurant dinners they share before driving back to Bricksburg each week. Oh, well, whatever works.

Ariel, Ariel. No matter what you think of her, she is one of the prettiest women ever seen in King County. Personally (thanks to Isabel), I am no longer confused by her wiles, yet I certainly understand how she is capable of confusing other guys. She's smart and she has a soul. It's not her fault that she looks like a fashion model, yet lives in a backwater boondocks. One day, I'm sure, Ariel will move on to a larger arena.

She and Virgil have been seeing a lot of each other since the night of her party. They go out on the weekends and walk together every day between classes at school. Isabel and I think Ariel and Virgil are suited as a couple; however, there is a tentative, not fully committed aura about their relationship. Ironically, it's Virgil who seems hesitant rather than Ariel, the reigning queen of fickle. I could say that she's receiving a dose of her own medicine; however, I believe Virgil is genuinely nebulous about the whole affair and is not trying to teach her a lesson. By the way, he recently cropped his hair to within an inch of his head and started growing a Fu Manchu. It's pretty cool. It makes him look like a philosophy student, which is what I guess he will be next year.

Margo Clay has been busy making changes along with the rest of us. First thing she did was dye her hair pink. Then she gave Harold Fassel his walking papers. After that she shocked the patrons of the Greasy Spoon with the announcement that she and Tiny were engaged to be married. I guess she's had all the fun she wants and is now ready to settle down. Good going, Tiny. Your persistence paid off.

And now *Persistence* with a capital *P*? My mother (without telling me she was doing so) submitted two hundred pages of her book to a literary agency in New York at the end of August. On the third of October she received a promising letter from someone claiming to be wildly enthusiastic about the work. Since then Mom and that someone (an agent named Prudence) have spoken twice on the phone and reached a working agreement. We're all just waiting now for Mom to finish the final chapter. She says she'll have it done before Christmas. I am happy for her, and extremely proud.

I wish I could wave my hand and tell you that Aunt June had a miraculous recovery from her mental illness, but unfortunately I'm not a wizard and I cannot do that. Yet I can report that her condition has not worsened, which is worth something, and I can also say that June has found a new hobby. She has recently taken to strolling the grounds of Western State Hospital, listening to birds. From what Louisa Bey tells Mom on the phone, June is already expert at identifying each species by its song, as well as interpreting the meaning of what the birds are singing. Good old June. I'm sure she understands their lyrics exactly.

Now for Isaac, who is the same as ever—not that I think he needs to change. With his outside-looking-in slant of mind, he's still the true-blue artist of Bricksburg . . . still the most unflap-pable guy in town. As for my relationship with his sister, he endorses it completely. In fact, he told me he always thought Isabel and I were cut out for each other and wondered when I'd wake up and smell the coffee. "Ha," I laughed, and asked him when he was going to wake up to Grace Cullighan. Typically, he was one step ahead of me. "Oh, didn't I tell you?" he replied as if the matter must have slipped his mind. "Grace and I have decided to move to New York together."

"When?"

"Next year, after we graduate. Grace wants to find work as a photographer in the fashion biz. She figures the earlier she gets started, the better."

"What about you? You going to be the next Andy Warhol?"

"Please, Cecil. Not that celebrity hound. He did more to pol-lute the river of art than just about anyone in this century. I just want to get a job in a coffee shop or something and paint during my free time. You know, do the poor artist thing."

Such statements seem to define Isaac. He can be fierce when it comes to ideas, but I don't believe there's an ounce of guile in him. He just wants to do art, and rather wisely, I think, he wants to do it with Grace at his side. She'll keep him straight. She'll see that he eats his vegetables and washes behind his ears.

Wow, look at the clock. It's two-thirty. My accelerator foot is itching. I wonder where Mom is with the car.

Patience, Cecil . . . finish the addendum. Don't forget Pauley Harrington's transformation from awkward misfit into debonair playboy. Maybe that's an exaggeration, yet it is true that Pauley and Itsy Nelson began dating after the night of Ariel's party, and then, after a month of going out with Itsy, Pauley started dating Itsy's best friend, Doreen Taylor. That also lasted for about a month, and now Pauley is back to dating Itsy. (Oddly enough, the friendship between Doreen and Itsy does not seem to have suffered from the back-and-forth developments.) Don't even ask me what's going on. I'd rather not speculate. I'm just glad Pauley is having fun.

Sadly, I must report that Bravo is still at large. Or at least no one in King County has seen the Harringtons' dog since he divorced himself from the family. I suppose, in a way, there is poetic justice in Bravo's story. I mean, whether you are a dog or a person, if you are going to have dignity and honor your beliefs, you must be willing to pay the price.

I hear a car door slam shut on the street. That must be Mom.

Before I leave off, let me just add: If you live anywhere east of the Mississippi River in the continental United States of America and you see a midsized rust-colored mutt with a crooked tail and the tip of its left ear missing, please treat that dog politely. It might be Bravo. And if it is, like all old people and all crazy people, he deserves every ounce of respect you have in your heart to give him.

Bye. Gotta go. Don't want to keep Isabel waiting.